The Apparition

John Wheatley

The Apparition

Contents

Chapter 1 — 1

Chapter 2 — 33

Chapter 3 — 39

Chapter 4 — 51

Chapter 5 — 57

Chapter 6 — 67

Chapter 7 — 75

Chapter 8 — 83

John's Yorkshire Titles — 93
John's Middleton Titles — 95
About the Author — 97
John's Anglesey titles — 99

1

Chapter 1

Anna, Staithes, 2010

If I'd realised how long the journey by train was going to take, I would probably have opted to drive, after all.

It was already beginning to get dark as we pulled out of Middlesborough. Two hours from Leeds to Middlesbrough, another two from Middlesbrough to Whitby, then a taxi from Whitby to Staithes. Definitely too much for a Friday night!

I should have driven. Or stayed at home.

What was it that persuaded me? The thought of reviving childhood memories, the romance of train journeys? Going on holiday to Scarborough or Filey; the competition to see who would be the first to see the sea? The excitement of it all, and a happiness so long forgotten it might almost never have existed.

I leaned my head back, closed my eyes and tried to snatch a quick doze but it was no use. *My weariness amazes me*, I muttered inside my head – one of my favourite Dylan lines: oh, the self-indulgence of being amazed by one's own weariness. My weariness did not feel luxurious or amazing, however. It was a hard, drained tiredness, with no Mr Tambourine Man to call on for a song!

I had gone straight to the station after my appointment with Madeline. Madeline was the solicitor handling my divorce. Madeline was thirty-two, though if you met her in any other context, you would think her much younger.

'We've had this,' Madeline said, producing a letter. 'From his solicitor. The usual stuff. Just have a read through and tell me what you think.'

The usual stuff, it seemed, was a litany of accusations and complaints.

'How can he say that?' I muttered aloud in disbelief.

'Oh don't worry about it, Anna. I'll draft a suitable reply. But I thought you should have sight of it. You see how it is, though. It's never nice. The aim is to intimidate you into agreeing a lesser settlement.'

'Can't I just do that anyway?'

'Mmm-nnn,' Madeline replied with an almost humorous intonation, synchronised with a shaking of the head. One way then the other, just once.

'So what are you up to at the weekend, then?' Madeline asked as we walked back through the office. Her tone had become light, very bright and chatty.

'Going up to Staithes, just further on from Whitby.'

'Nice!' said Madeline with exaggerated approval. 'Get away from it all for a bit. Just what you need!'

Opening my eyes from the futile attempt to drop off, I wondered now, as the train slid on through the evening, what Madeline did at the weekend. I could easily picture her in one of those trendy and ever-so-slightly exclusive wine or gin bars high above the city, all glass and sky terraces. Not someone to get snarled up in the kind of mess I was in. Though no doubt divorce solicitors go through divorces too.

I also wondered again if this whim of a trip up to Staithes was such a good idea after all. Might it not have been more relaxing to stay at home – a long shower, something decent from M&S to microwave, a bottle of wine, an early night. Last week I had said to myself, if I have to spend one more Friday like this, I shall go mad! Now, it seemed much the preferable option.

The cottage at Staithes, near the harbour of the old fishing village, once belonged to an aunt, or a great-aunt, we sometimes visited when I was little, when we were on holiday. Just a flying day visit as the cottage was far too small for all of us to stay in. I could hardly remember the old lady, but I remembered liking it when dad took me down to the harbour to see the boats and the nets and the lobster pots.

And then, somehow, decades later, the cottage had come to me, not directly through a will but simply because they had traced me as the last remaining relative. Martin – the husband from whom I was currently being divorced – had seized control. My own inclination had been to sell it and to use the money to support my little newly fledged business, but Martin would not hear of it. 'A little gold-mine,' he insisted, and in a sense he was right, because it had hardly ever wanted for holiday lets during the main months of the season. It was not really the money that Martin had been interested in, though. Something had rankled in him at the thought of putting money into my business venture. I gave way – as I always did.

Thankfully, a taxi was waiting at the station in Whitby, and thankfully it was a driver who, apart from basic courtesy, showed no wish to engage in chatter. It took twenty-five minutes, and then we were heading down the steep road towards the lower part of the village. The driver took me to the foot of the Barrass steps, as near to the cottage as it was possible to get by car, then, leaving me with my weekend case and my lap-top in its shoulder bag, pulled away to do the circuit around the bottom of the village.

Staithes, I should explain, for anyone who does not know of it, is a coastal village squeezed between two massive cliff faces, at the foot of a deep ravine through which Staithes Beck finds its way to the sea. In summer weather, it resembles one of those picturesque fishing villages found along mountainous stretches of coasts of the Mediterranean, with the appeal of higgledy-piggledy dwellings cast seemingly one on top of the other up the hillside, interlaced by narrow passageways, cobbled alleys and twisting stone staircases. Of course, the climate of the east coast of Yorkshire is not that of the Mediterranean, and for many months of the year it is beset by wind and rain, high seas, tempest, and sheer cold. It used to be a fishing village pure and simple, but all that has long gone, and instead, its charms, despite the sometimes inclement weather, have turned it into a popular seaside resort.

As I have said, the nearest the taxi could get me was the foot of the Barrass steps, sometimes locally known as 'Sliptop'. At the top of the eight wide steps, a small flagged and cobbled square, with cottages on each side, slopes upwards for thirty metres – with a handrail set along the middle, presumably to assist those in danger of slipping, and then disperses into a number of passages, steps and ginnels, and a turn to the left and a twist to the left brings you to my cottage.

The Nook is, I have to admit, even by Staithes standards, tiny, though on Booking.com it qualifies as 'bijou'. There is a single room downstairs, just big enough for a settee, an armchair and a small dining table, and there is a little extension which is just big enough to contain a kitchen, with fridge, cooker, sink and a short length of worktop. A staircase with two turns brings you to the bedroom with double bed, wardrobe and dressing table; and then the bathroom is above the kitchen. Because the cottage is on the upwards part of the slope from the village, the bedroom window affords a view out over the corner of some other pantile rooftops towards the corner of the harbour. With the window open, at night you can hear the wash of the tide below.

During the first winter, I had builders in to refurbish the whole cottage which had fallen into a pretty sad state. Much of the work was re-plastering, roof and chimney repair, re-wiring etc.; the only structural change I made, was to create a new porch and front door, the previous door being into a cramped alley to the side, which at that time opened with a latch and an old iron key. I left the iron key, mainly for show, as the mortice was quite rusty and clunky, and for security had a heavy bolt put in place.

It became something a pet project for a while and having won the battle of sell/not sell, Martin was quite happy for me to have my little project. Apart from the porch and new doorway, I tried to retain as many of the original features as possible, the sash windows, internal doors with latches, stone fireplace with oak beam. I went around car-boot sales in Leeds and sourced some period items, a brass bedframe, a small stove to sit in the fireplace, two vintage candle lanterns each a metre high. Also, some oak furniture pieces and a wooden table complete with designer wormholes. The delivery men were not well pleased when they saw how many steps they had to climb, but I smiled sweetly, promised a cup of tea, and they knuckled down to it with a good grace.

The only other thing – and this I realised the first time I stayed there – was the need to have a landline installed, there being

absolutely no mobile phone signal whatsoever in Staithes!

So, having dragged myself, my weekend case and my lap-top up Slip-top, I let myself in and all but collapsed into a chair. I had been promising myself a glass of wine all through the journey, but the wine I'd brought wasn't chilled, and I decided after a few sips that it wasn't going to do me any good, so I simply unpacked the essentials, and went to bed.

I didn't sleep well that first night. The truth is that I never sleep that well the first night away from my own bed, and my frequent wakeful episodes were punctuated with weird dreams as if someone had folded some toxic concoction into the undercurrents of my sleeping consciousness. I had been aware of wind and rain during the night, and when I finally woke up to the grey light of day, I could see that the weather was still filthy. It was certainly not what I'd been hoping for. I curled up, loath to get out of bed, remembering those long-ago days of youth when I could happily lie in bed on Saturday morning until noon.

Then the phone rang. I checked caller-ID and was relieved to see that it was not Stella, my daughter, or any other member of my family, especially not Martin. In fact, it was Jenny from work.

'How is it?' she asked, bright and chirpy as ever.

I sat up on the side of the bed and tried to make myself sound alert and fully functioning.

'Fine,' I replied, 'Weather a bit dodgy.'

'Same here. Anyway, I just called to let you know that order from Franks did come in.'

'Oh good.'

'Only just mind you!'

'So, we can crack on Monday morning, then.'

My company is a business making bespoke up-market cards and stationery. I started it ten years ago when Stella flew the nest. Very small to begin with, just me, Jenny dealing with orders and deliveries, and Geoff, fresh from uni who brought with him all the tech savvy we needed for an online service.

'OK, then,' said Jenny. 'I'll leave you to it. Don't do anything crazy!'

'No chance of that!'

Right, then, I said to myself, now jumping up and pulling on my dressing gown. Kettle. Coffee. Toast. The wind was still swirling about the house as I ate my breakfast, but I was now determined not to be put off. I pulled on my jeans and a sweater, the most sensible boots I'd been able to find, a hooded waterproof coat that had probably once belonged to Stella, and an old bobble-cap. And off I set.

I rounded the bottom of the village, past the Cod and Lobster – where I could remember sitting whilst my dad had a pint – and then set out up Church Street past the little houses until the road became a steep gravelly track leading upwards, with what looked like a gorge falling steeply away to the right. I came eventually, a little out of breath, to a farm, and then followed the path between fields to the cliff-top from which I could see the village, looking very picturesque, in spite of the weather, almost like a toytown, below.

The wind was now gusting and tugging at my coat as if it had every intention of ripping it off my back, and the sea looked disturbed the way you imagine a nervous breakdown to be, troubled all the way to a smudged and dirty horizon under a fast-moving sky. Nevertheless, inspired by my own boldness in getting so far, I resolved to go further. The path ran at a safe enough distance, along the line of the cliff, bordered by a fence whose meaning was clear enough, for the drops beyond seemed absolutely sheer.

Sometimes, for a few moments, as if I had walked into some natural declivity which formed a shelter, the wind seemed to ease into a pocket of calm, only to gust and buffet again a moment later with relentless force, driving the very breath back into my mouth if I turned on to it the wrong way. I strode on, telling myself that this confrontation with unleashed nature was exactly the liberating force I needed. I wondered if, like King Lear on the wild heath, I should start tearing off my clothes... well, of course, I didn't really wonder that, but what I did feel, cold and blown about as I was, was exactly the kind of mood changing experience I had been hoping for when I decided to break out of the dull monotony of my usual Leeds weekend.

I walked on another mile, maybe two. I was vaguely aware from looking at one of the walk books that we had provided for visitors to the cottage, that if I carried on along the coast path – the Cleveland Way – I would come to another bay with a village, Port Mulgrave at its head, and that from there I could work my way back by another path inland, or if all else failed by the road.

It is when you come into view of these bays – there are several along the stretch of coast – that you realise the staggering beauty of the headlands and cliff formations, especially on a day like this, with the sea pounding against the rocks and sending up huge sprays of boiling surf.

I walked on and on. Further than I should have done really, given my untrained walking state, but under some sort of compulsion. I passed occasionally another walker, or usually a pair of walkers and we hailed each other heartily and made sardonic remarks about the weather. I reached the next bay along which I knew must be Runswick Bay and it was there that the sky suddenly broke open, in a gash of blue through which lemon sunshine struck like a blinding searchlight. All the colours changed. The sea, the sand, the craggy rocks suddenly had a different personality and I just wanted to sit down and take it all in. I found a convenient slab of rock, sat down , and looked over the view, down to the sands and the cliffs, maybe a mile away, and the sea, and for a moment I had one of those deja-vu moments, the feeling that I'd seen it before and knew it in very precise way, though I couldn't pinpoint it at all, however much I tried. I stayed for twenty minutes, not just because of the beauty of the view, and not just because my brain was trying to fathom its own strange reaction, but because the aches and pains in my calves and ankles were beginning to require it. I set off back, more slowly than my striding out. When I got back, I had been out for seven hours. I promised myself something nice – a piping hot cup of tea, a takeaway from the Cobbles, a glass of now chilled wine – what I did was put my head back and drift into a sleep.

I don't know how long I slept, probably not more than a couple of minutes, a kind of dreamy half-sleep I suppose you might call it, but it was the buzz of the phone which brought me back to full consciousness. I let it buzz on for what seemed an inordinately long time until at last it went still. Then I got up, and checked to find, as I'd suspected, that it was Stella's number. I love my daughter dearly but one of the reasons I'd come up here was precisely to get away from the awkwardness of the kind of phone-call I'd been having with her recently.

Stella, now 28, is, like her father, a dentist. She lives in Manchester where she trained, with Guy, her partner, also a dentist. Having carved out a very nice life for herself, the last thing Stella wants is to see her parents bickering, as she sees it, like irresponsible adolescents. She would like everything in the garden at home to be rosy, I suppose, so that she can be free to cultivate her own garden.

Rob, my son, two years younger than Stella, living in London and trying to make his way in the world of accountancy, had made it pretty plain that he simply didn't want to know.

I put the kettle on, but before I could make the cup of tea I was gasping for, the buzzing of the phone started again. Once more I was inclined to let it run its course, but then I remembered, with an internally muttered 'damn!' the anxiety I always felt when, during her student days, Stella didn't pick up her phone.

'Hi mum. Tried to call you just now. Why didn't you pick up?'

'Sorry,' I lied, 'I was in the shower.'

'I just thought I'd give you a quick call, see how you are.'

'I'm fine,' I replied. 'Absolutely fine.'

'Are you sure?'

'Of course. You don't need to worry about me. I told you.'

I had told her I was planning this weekend away, hoping to drop the hint that I didn't really want to be disturbed.

'Dad's here,' she said.

I quickly re-set all my dials. It was immediately obvious that this call had been Martin's idea. She hadn't even said the 'dad's here' bit sotto voce. I could see him standing there a few feet away, listening in, the silent master of ceremonies.

'Will you have a word with him?'

'No,' I said.

'Why not?'

'Because I'm away for the weekend to relax, darling, and because I don't want to.'

There was a guilt-making silence at the other end.

'And because there would be no point. Has he put you up to this?'

'No,' she said unconvincingly. 'It was my idea. I can't see why you just don't talk to each other, why you can't just try to sort something out.'

'Is that what your dad says, that we could just try to sort something out?'

'Well, at least he thinks you should try. Maybe he's right. I mean, you've been together for nearly thirty years and now you're chucking it all away.'

I terminated the call in the most calm and controlled way I could, but inside I was neither calm nor controlled. I decided to forego the cup of tea and go straight on to the glass of wine. It helped me to resolve my feelings into distinct strands, the main strand being anger at Martin's attempt to use Stella to manipulate the situation, and the other strands being, for the most part, derivatives from that.

After about twenty minutes, I resumed my thoughts at a practical level with regard to my arrangements for the evening. I had thought of going along to the pub for half an hour, but that had gone by the board now, if for no other reason than that I could not be bothered making the effort to make myself look presentable. I pulled my ordinary coat on and went along the way to the Cobbles and chose, guess what, a microwave dinner, and took two bottles of Chardonnay from the chiller section and added those to my basket. No point in running short!

It was now dark, but the weather had changed completely. I walked a little way along the harbour. The tide was in, and a few boats were bobbing about just below. The wind had dropped and there were open patches in the sky where stars seemed to be crowding into view. It helped me re-set my dials again. I began to look forward to my little boozy night alone.

Underneath, of course, I felt sorry for Stella. She was in the middle of it through no fault of her own, and I knew that she cared for both of us and was hurt by what was going on. She had always been something of a daddy's-little-girl, and I couldn't expect her to see Martin as I saw him, or to feel about him as I felt. I didn't want her to. And I certainly didn't want her to be snagged up in the middle of it.

The worst of it – and this had been part of my reaction both during and after the phone-call – was the feeling that maybe it really was all down to me. The suspicion that crawls out of the undergrowth and is suddenly upon you, that you are the one who has got things all out of proportion, that you, for some flimsy and barely articulate motive of selfishness, are the one who is making everyone else's life a misery.

The truth is that I did find it difficult to express my reasons for leaving Martin and wanting a divorce. When I had first seen her Madeline put me through a kind of catechism:

Physical abuse?

No.

Mental cruelty?

As in?

Unreasonable behaviour. Could be any number of things.

Can I think about it?

OK. Sexual abuse?

No.

Neglect?

We were both aware of a long pause after the question that could have been a question mark in its own right. I didn't try to answer it.

Can't I just say that I no longer love him?

Well, you can, but his people will try to argue unreasonableness on your part.

Why did I find it so difficult to give direct answers to these questions? Maybe it's just me. I mean, I even find it difficult to answer those 'customer satisfaction' questionnaires when you've bought something on-line. Sometimes the offered answers just don't reflect what I'm actually thinking; either that or else I refrain from saying what I really think in case I say something that will spoil someone else's business prospects. I know that I am always really glum when anyone says anything less than 'fantastic' on our customer website. But maybe it's different when it comes to a marriage satisfaction questionnaire.

I don't know at what point my mind started to drift into wider circles. Probably after about three quarters of a bottle of wine, by which time my anger and anxiety had dissipated.

I recalled a conversation I had had with Jenny earlier in the week. I think it was apropos of me saying that I had had a thoroughly boring weekend, that Jenny had asked: 'Have you ever thought of going on a dating site?'

'I'm 49, Jenny,' I said, 'not 29.'

If I was waiting for a compliment about my youthful looks and trim figure, Jenny evidently did not feel the need to make it. Instead, 'there are dating sites for middle aged people,' was her reply. 'For all sorts of people, these days. Whatever floats your boat. It's a big business.'

'I'm going through a divorce,' I countered.

'Would that make any difference, legally, I mean?'

'Probably not.'

'On the other hand, I suppose you wouldn't want anyone to think you were on the rebound, would you? Might be a bit of a turn-off.'

Jenny had a way of putting things that sometimes got straight to the point, but in this instance, it was more the case that I simply couldn't bear the thought of going through any process that involved talking about myself in any kind of romantic context. I had no idea how dating sites worked but I supposed that it must involve tentative exchanges of personal information and then what must amount to a semi-blind date, with the prospect of it being entirely awful, and I simply baulked at the whole idea of it.

'What about the sex, though?' Jenny bowled in with next. 'Don't you miss that?'

'Not really,' I replied, trying to drop a dead bat on it. Whenever Martin wanted sex, which wasn't often, I felt as if I was an old sweater he'd found in a drawer and thought he might as well wear. Apart from that my sex life for the last ten years had consisted mainly of infrequent and forlorn instances of solitary gratification, usually hedged about by feelings of inadequacy and a mild sense of shame.

'I suppose it does leave you eventually,' said Jenny, wistfully. 'The sex urge, I mean. Difficult to imagine though.'

Without actually boasting, Jenny had a way of letting everyone know that she and her partner Tom enjoyed a full and hearty sex life.

The bottle of wine which I had opened the previous night was now empty and I made no bones about opening another. It was only quarter to ten, and I was pleased enough with my exertions of the day to feel like extending the celebration a little longer. Had I been at home I might have put on the television and looked for something on Netflix, but it felt cosy in the cottage's little sitting room, and for once I was quite happy with my own company. I did check my phone every five minutes or so, an ingrained habit, though now the lack of Wi-Fi meant that the usual perplexity of incoming information was curtailed and I was glad of that. I had also brought my lap-top in in case I felt the inclination to do some work, but no such inclination came, and after a couple more glasses of wine I was content to let my thoughts remain in the realm of vague reverie. Finally, I remembered to plug in both my lap-top and my phone to recharge, and dragged myself, more tipsy than I had thought, up the narrow staircase and into bed.

I was woken, in the morning, by an odd but distinct noise, and at first I couldn't work out whether the noise had penetrated my sleep from an external source or whether it had been part of a dream that had suddenly snapped me awake. I sat up on one elbow and listened. For a few moments there was nothing; I was about to rest my head back on the pillow, becoming conscious that I was also suffering some symptoms of a hangover, when the noise came again, a scraping noise, the sound a chair makes when you knock into it. Immediately I felt a sense of tense alarm at the thought that someone else was in the house. For a moment, alert in every nerve for further sounds, I dared not move, let alone get out of bed. Had I been so drunk last night that I had forgotten to push the bolt closed on the back door? I remembered going out to put some rubbish in the bin, but I was sure I had bolted the door when I came back, could even picture the moment of doing it, but how else could a stranger have got into the house?

I waited, I don't know how long, probably just seconds, for a further noise but none came, and at last, I moved first one foot and then the other out of the bed, and straining not to make any noise myself, stood up. Then I moved, silent step by silent step towards the top of the stairs.

'Hello?' I called, feebly, aware of the wobble in my own voice.

There was no reply.

I put one foot onto the first stair and then another. It was then I heard the click of the latch and something in my stomach curdled, paralysing me again for a few seconds. Then, with a sudden access of do-or-die adrenalin, I strode down the stairs and into the kitchen. No-one was there but the back door was ajar, as if someone had just made an exit. I looked at the place on the door where I was sure I had locked the bolt, just to confirm the muscle memory of having done it, but strange as it seemed, there was no bolt there at all, just the latch.

I went straight across to the door and looked out into the little yard behind. Nothing. I went a few steps further to the cobbled lane and looked in the direction of the harbour. There, perhaps twenty yards further on, I saw a figure, cloaked and hooded, carrying, over its shoulder, something that looked like a leather bag.

'Hey!' I called after her. It could have been a woman or it could have been a child, I couldn't really work out the size relative to the perspective, but I was sure it was a female. 'Hey!'

The figure made no response. She neither turned at the sound of being called, nor did she seem to hurry. I began to follow, sure that what she was carrying had been stolen from the house, but after I had gone a few yards, the figure turned, and was out of my immediate sight. When I came to where she had last been, there was nothing. I looked this way and that, I went on another twenty yards trying to work out exactly how she had managed to dodge me, and then stopped.

There was, thank goodness, no-one else about; but it was after six o'clock in the morning, and here I was, barefoot and in nothing but my nightdress, wandering near the harbour in a thin drizzle, to all intents and purposes like someone who has gone out of her mind.

I hurried back, and once in the safety of the house I did a hasty inventory. My laptop and phone were still there charging, exactly as I had left them; if my visitor had been an opportunistic thief, then surely they would have been snapped up. The same with my handbag – there it was on the table, and in it my purse, packed with credit cards and cash. All untouched.

Could it be, I wondered, that I had managed to disturb the thief just in time?

I tried to remember what else, besides my own immediate possessions had been there. As far as I could tell everything was present and correct, the toaster, the kettle, the television, even the two tell-tale empty bottles on the draining board. And there was nothing I could recall that in any way resembled the leather bag, or whatever it was the figure had been carrying.

I had been avoiding looking at the place where the bolt had been – or not been - but now steeling myself to do so, I saw that it was there. This might have been a source of relief, because the absence of the bolt had been in some ways the scariest bit of the whole episode, but what added to my general consternation was that it was now firmly in the locked position, and I had no recollection, having re-entered not more than a minute ago, of having locked it myself. This confirmed to me that something seriously weird was happening, and that it was probably happening inside my head.

I began to experience symptoms that were very similar to a migraine: lights getting in the way of my direct vision, a growing headache, feelings of dizziness and sickness. I groped my way back up the stairs and into bed.

Where I must have slept, for when I opened my eyes again it was nearly nine o'clock, and, though the symptoms of my migraine had gone, I still felt shaky. For a few moments, I tried to persuade myself that I had dreamt the whole thing, but then I saw that my nightdress was on the floor and remembered that I had pulled it off because it was wet from the drizzle outside. To confirm this, when I picked it up, it was still damp.

I quickly dressed, and went downstairs, warily glancing at the locked bolt as I got into the kitchen. There was nothing further amiss. I put the kettle on, which seemed to be the first step towards a return to normality, and made a cup of coffee. Then, I switched on my laptop to check through my emails, and put on the television to have the reassuringly normal Andrew Marr show on in the background.

Later, with still nothing further to disturb my serenity, and finding it possible to push earlier events to the vaguer recesses of my mind, I called a taxi and went to wait for it outside the pub. I have a horror of being late for taxis and the like, so I tend to go to the other extreme and leave bags of time. Consequently, I had a full quarter of an hour to wait, but it had turned into a pleasant enough early afternoon so I didn't mind. It was there, as I was waiting, that I came across Arnold.

I had seen a small fishing boat coming in and had watched it in an absent-minded as the owner tied it to the moorings. This turned out to be Arnold.

He came up towards the pub as if he might be heading there for a pint, and nodded to me. 'Staying in the village?' he asked in a downbeat way, politeness rather than curiosity.

'Just leaving,' I replied. 'Waiting for a taxi.'

He nodded.

'Been fishing?'

He nodded again.

'Catch anything?'

'No. Be fish fingers for tea again.'

'You live here?'

He nodded, then, 'Arnold Stead,' he announced.

I would have returned the introduction but just then a car-horn sounded.

'Your taxi,' he said, and as I made my way round, he headed into the pub.

It turned out to be one of those weeks. The delivery which had come in late on Friday now became a full-on job due to go out to a wedding client before the end of the week, and we had two further orders on the go. Consequently, there was not much time to sit around and chat, and I spent a good bit of the day on the phone to other customers and suppliers. I had called my doctor, Miriam, first thing and had made an appointment for 5pm. It is perhaps a sign of my insecurity that whenever anything happens that stirs my propensity for anxiety, I feel the need to run things by other people, professional people. So, because I needed her reassurance, I booked in to see Miriam, but by dinner time I was wishing I hadn't. Amidst the thread and thrum of a working day in Leeds it had come to seem superfluous. I felt perfectly normal. How-ever, having made the appointment I thought I'd better go.

I like Miriam. She has a way of listening that somehow gives you con-fidence, shrewd and entirely non-judgemental.

I told her the tale of my weird Sunday morning experience, and it al-most seemed that she heard stories of ghostly figures and disappearing door bolts on a daily basis. She nodded her head sagely until I came to the end.

'So what do you think?' I asked, determined to offer the possibility of treating it at the level of a joke. 'Do you think I'm going off my trol-ley?'

Miriam smiled. 'Not at all,' she said warmly. 'If you take one or two little details out, it becomes a perfectly ordinary set of circumstances. It may be that someone popped their head in at the door. Maybe expect-ing to find someone else there. Nothing was taken, you say?'

'No.'

'Well, I imagine someone seeing your laptop and things realised their mistake and popped back out again pretty sharp.'

It was my turn to nod, as I fitted all this into place. 'What about the bolt being not there?'

'You say you passed it by quickly.'

'Yes, I wanted to see who it was.'

'And it was there when you came back in?'

'Yes.'

'You were in a bit of a panic as anyone would be hearing someone in the house. Your immediate thought was that you'd forgotten to push the bolt to. For a split second you imagined the bolt wasn't there.'

I was prepared to believe this. The memory had already lost some of its original clarity and I couldn't have sworn on the bible that the bolt was absolutely not there. The same was true of the figure disappearing. If it was someone from the village, a child or teenager, she would know how to nip out of sight pretty quick if she thought she was being chased.

'So you think it's all an over-reaction?'

Miriam smiled her warm supportive smile again, the one where she is really smiling from the eyes. 'I wouldn't say that, not at all. But we know you've been under quite a bit of strain, with one thing and another.'

'Yes.'

'Let's see,' she said, turning to her computer screen. 'You had a course of anti-depressants a few years ago.'

'Yes, that was Dr Kay.'

'And how was that?'

'Made me feel very light-headed for a few days.' I shrugged my shoulders, and didn't say anything else.

'I get the feeling you don't want to go down that route again.'

'Not really.'

'OK. Well, you seem quite calm about it all now. Let's see how it goes for a few days. If you get anxious or anything, just call the surgery and I can do you a prescription on-line.'

I left feeling glad, after all, that I had gone. Miriam had pretty much confirmed that I wasn't going round the bend, and that was good enough for me.

I was glad that I had resisted any temptation to go back on anti-depressants. I suppose they must have done something to help me back then – it must have been eight or nine years ago - but what I remembered most was Martin's *what on earth do you need those for* attitude, and I suppose that had distilled in me the view that anti-depressants were somehow the 'weakness' drug. I took plenty of other drugs: ibuprofen, paracetamol, codeine occasionally, the odd sleeping pill, and I suppose you would have to add alcohol to that list, but they were somehow the 'coping' drugs, and for a long time, especially now, I had needed to believe that I was coping.

I hadn't made any plans for going back to Staithes. The following weekend there was a booking – even during the cold wet windy months the cottage does a fair trade – and anyway I needed to catch up with my paperwork, which is often the case after a busy week. It was the weekend after that, when I got a sudden cancellation, that I decided to have another break by the sea. This time, I loaded up the car and I was there by seven thirty. Of course, you can't really park in the village unless you are one of the lucky few who has a space but you can pull over for long enough to unload, which I did, before taking the car up to the car-park above the village.

As I walked down the steep lane back to the village, I was still mulling over a telephone conversation with Madeline, the one that had been buzzing about in my head all through the journey.

'We need to talk about assets,' she said.

'I thought I'd told you. Did I miss something?'

'No. I mean his assets. We need to thrash it out.'

'In what sense?'

'I think we should go for a 60-40 split,' said Madeline.

'How's that?'

'60-40 - in your favour.'

Well, I have to admit that even to me 60-40 seemed a bit unfair. I vaguely thought we'd split it down the middle. And after all, I was the one who had left the family home.

'I know what you're going to say,' said Madeline, intercepting my re-action, 'but listen. He will have a pension, a big pension. What were you doing for twenty years when he was building up that pension? Bringing up his kids.'

'I did work a bit,' I replied.

'Yes, but you paid a married woman's tax rate. I'm only going off what you said. That may well will affect your state pension. I know your business is doing OK now but it might not always be so. He may have other investments, other pensions that you will miss out on.'

'I don't really want any of his pensions. I just want to be completely free of him.'

'I quite understand, but that's why we've got to go for 60-40, at least.'

'OK.'

'And I can tell you this, if they accept it, it's because they know it's in his best interest.'

'And if they don't?'

'We'll go after his pension. Say we want half of all his pensions, and then wrangle.'

'It all sounds very adversarial,' I said.

'Look, as far as I can tell, you've been living with a very controlling man for thirty years, maybe you don't see it as clearly as an outsider might, but there is certainly no need for you to feel guilty about it.'

'Guilt is my middle name,' I said.

'Well, dear, we are just going to have to change that.'

It was true, and I knew it, that I had a guilt habit; that things never felt right unless I had something to feel wrong about, but it was also true that I was the one who had walked out of the family home.

Of course, as soon as he found out where I was, Martin came round. I was more or less expecting it – something I had to go through sooner or later.

'What on earth is going on?' he said, in a more in sorrow than anger sort of mode.

'I needed to get away. Get some space.'

He let out a long sigh. 'You don't answer my calls, I've texted you, I've e-mailed you. Nothing. Now is that fair? By any standard?'

'I'm sorry,' I said, hearing the old weakness in my voice. 'I just didn't know what to say.'

'But surely now, if at no other time in your life, you should have a clear sense of what you want to say.'

'I've already said it.'

'By that I suppose you mean that note. Three sentences, if that. Don't you think I'm entitled to a little more than that?'

'I didn't want to get into an argument. Like this.'

'Asking for a reasonable explanation is not an argument.'

He waited for me to reply. Nothing came.

'I think you're not well,' he said, at last.

'I'm all right. I'm fine.'

'Look I don't blame you,' he went on. 'I understand how you feel. But this is just going too far. I want you to think it over. Stay here for a couple of weeks, if you like. OK. Give yourself a bit of space. I'll stay out of your hair. Give it two weeks.'

'I've got a lease for six months.'

'It doesn't matter. We can pay it off.'

Again, I didn't reply. I was aware all the time of how flimsy my explanations would sound.

'Are you having an affair?' he asked suddenly. 'Is that it?'

'No.'

'If you are...'

'I'm not.'

'This just isn't making any sense to me. I really don't understand what you want.'

'I want a divorce.'

He banged his fist on the table. Martin very rarely gets angry but when he does it is with an abrupt burst that can be quite frightening.

'I think I want you to go now,' I said, feeling close to tears and knowing that he would try to exploit my tears with false consolation. I've never been good at expressing things in an argument with him. If I don't want to give in, I have to resort to silence. Usually I just give in.

He strode around the room showing no sign of having heard what I said. 'Look, I'm sorry,' he said at last, holding up his hands. 'Didn't mean to lose my rag. I'm just... I'm really concerned. Genuinely, I'm worried about you.'

'You don't need to be.'

'I've seen this coming on,' he said. 'You've never been the same since you started that business. It's too much.'

'It's nothing to do with the business,' I said, meekly.

'Look, see your doctor. Promise me you'll see your doctor. Maybe some of those tablet things you used to take.'

I had decided now to stay in the safety of my silent mode.

He left eventually but I felt demoralised and unsure of myself. For as long as I could remember, things that went wrong or fell short of expectation could usually be traced back to something I'd done or hadn't done. It didn't even need Martin to point it out anymore. It had become my habitual way of thinking.

Once, at a dinner party not long after we were married, someone referred to me, in a slightly tongue-in-cheek way, as the 'perfect' wife. It was partly meant as a compliment, and though I was aware that it had connotations of submissiveness, I didn't mind at all. It was an image I accepted. I'd known since I was fifteen or sixteen that I had my fair share of the things that men find attractive, and I didn't try to take any moral high ground by insisting that there was more to being a woman than having a nice face and a nice figure. I was flattered and I liked it.

Nor did I question the idea that the husband should be the stronger partner in a marriage, the one responsible for the big decisions. Once, before we were engaged, I went to St Anne's near Blackpool for the weekend with some friends and a couple of boys. There was nothing untoward going on, it was just that one of the boys had a car and his parents had an apartment there. It so happened that Martin came home from college that weekend. When he found out, he came over and fetched me home. Of course, I was annoyed at the time that he had interrupted what amounted to nothing more than a bit of innocent fun, but my mother, speaking up for him, said it demonstrated how serious he was. Both my father and my mother liked Martin. He was a dental student and everyone knew that dentists earned a lot of money. He was a good prospect.

We were engaged a few months later, just before I went to college, and I stayed faithful to him all through my course. The summer I finished, we got married. For a while after that, when I was teaching, I kept up my hobby of painting – art had been one of my subjects in training – and in our first place, a flat in Kirkstall, some of my pictures went on the wall; he indulged me the way you would a child with its first infant attempts: *well done, darling, come here, let me give you a cuddle, let me give you a fondle, let's hop into bed.* By the time we bought the house in Yeadon, the days of the walls being ornamented with my art were long in the past, as was any enthusiasm I might once have had for it.

In the early years, Martin had two affairs (that I know of) one with a receptionist, also married, and another with one of the numerous young dental nurses who came and went. Just flings he said. Just happened. Means nothing. There was no-one I could really talk to. I felt a sense of shame and failure. I could have left him but realised I was more scared of being alone than living with a husband who had been unfaithful. Besides I had a young child. I slept in a separate room for three weeks. Then, at some point, normal service resumed. Martin had persuaded me that I was the one who was being unreasonable. Soon after that Rob was on the way.

If I had found out about his carryings-on in the usual grubby ways – checking his emails, checking his phone after the calls he had stepped out of the room to take, etc. - after that I stopped checking. I didn't want to know. Not knowing gave me a veneer of self-protection; I could live in my own cocoon.

But we did all the things a family does. Holidays abroad. Christmas and birthday celebrations. In some ways he was a very good dad. He had us all in his thrall. He played hockey for a local team into his thirties, then golf. When he became the Golf Club Captain, he dragged me along to the socials which I pretended to enjoy. He was Mr Popular, the man who made funny speeches, the man who was good at everything.

I don't know quite when, but at some point I realised that I had nothing that was my own.

It was then, when Stella went to uni and Rob was doing his A levels, that I decided to start my business.

As I became more independent, things in the marriage got worse. He didn't like my independence. To begin with it was, on the surface at least, protective: he didn't want me to fall flat on my face, to be disappointed by failure, to be upset, to be stressed. It was never to do with money, though as I've said, when I put up the idea of selling the cottage to invest in the business, he moved fast to head me off at the pass.

Sometimes, it was his outwardly gentle humour that cut me to the quick. I remember him saying, at one golf social, 'my lovely wife has embarked on a project of monetising her craft skills – and I'm sure you will all agree that the sum of human happiness will be greatly enhanced thereby...' This elicited easy and not ill-intentioned mirth in the committee room where we were, but I had to hide my embarrassment. And it was true: he did add to the sum of happiness in a tangible way – he repaired teeth, took away pain, did root canals and implants; beside that I felt useless.

At home the humour wasn't always quite so gentle. I remember telling him once that I was going to be late home.

'What on earth for?' he asked.

'We've got a lot on,' I explained.

'Oh per-lease,' he muttered under his breath, in the sense of saying, I'm only being supremely reticent about this out of consideration for you, but really, come on, you are kidding yourself.

'I've put the dinner on timer,' I said, still feeling the need to defer to my other role.

It was a typical conversation.

And then, one night, nearly four months ago, I decided to leave. He was away at the time, on a conference of some kind, and I thought the unthinkable. Had I really sifted through the complexities I probably wouldn't have done it, but I didn't think it through at all. As if it was an adventure, I found a flat, took a six-month lease, left a note, phoned the kids, and moved.

He accused me of being secretive and devious. I suppose I was. Otherwise, I couldn't have done it.

I finished my drink and switched on the TV just to get the news headlines. I could easily have opened another bottle of wine and stayed up, but in the end, I decided to go to bed, and as soon as I got in I was glad that I had. It was raining again outside, but in a way it was soothing, and sleepiness quickly crept over me.

When I next awoke it was still dark, and I could hear the distant rhythm of the sea with its endless slow motion, back and forth. The rain had now stopped, and it was peaceful. I knew that I'd slept deeply, my body felt luxuriously relaxed and suffused with a kind of mild yearning. I listened to the sea for a while and it seemed that time with all its distinctions, might be suspended, almost dissolved. I need not go into detail, but later, gently cast ashore, you could say, on the tide of my own pleasure, I closed my eyes in grateful relief and slept again.

I felt better in the morning than I could remember feeling for a long time, and I was up and about before eight o'clock. I indulged myself in scrambled eggs for breakfast and made a cafetiere of coffee rather than just settling for instant. Afterwards I spread the OS map I had bought in town out on the table and had a look. I am not normally very good with maps – I am one of those people who probably could not exist without a sat-nav – but I was obviously able to see the line of the coast and to pick out the places I already knew. I could also trace the route of the walk I had taken on my previous visit.

I spent a little time just walking round the village. It is only a small place but there are some interesting nooks and crannies. I had more or less dismissed my encounter of two weeks before as of no significance, whatever its explanation, but I could still recall, with amusement, the ridiculous figure I must have cut, standing there in the rain. I took a few photographs on my phone: the harbour, the line of fishermen's cottages that made up most of the village, the little bridge over the Staithes Beck which crosses to the other side of the harbour, under the cliffs.

In the afternoon, I drove over to Sandsend, another pretty little place just along the coast. When I got back, I decided that I would like to eat somewhere where there were a few more people, so I called in at the pub and reserved a table for myself at 7.30pm.

There were half a dozen drinkers, and two couples having a meal when I arrived. It was a quiet atmosphere, not too off-putting for a woman on her own. A young girl, very friendly, took me to a table and brought me a menu. I asked for a glass of Pinot Grigio and sat back to relax. The walls were decorated with old black and white photographs of the village, and later, when I had finished eating, I took a closer look at them.

Several were of the pub itself, and it was clear that the 'The Cod and Lobster' was not just a catchy modern name but one which went back probably to a time before tourists were the mainstay of the economy. One which caught my attention showed a kind of parade in the town, sometime in the 1950s, and behind, straddling the entire valley was what looked like a huge railway viaduct. Others had been taken around the harbour and its surrounds at various states of the tide and weather.

'Gets pretty stormy at times.'

I turned to the speaker to see that it was the man who had introduced himself to me as Arnold, a couple of weeks ago.

'Looks wild,' I replied. 'I bet you don't go out in your boat when it's like that.'

'Not a chance!' he grinned, from his stool at the bar.

The girl was bringing the tab I had asked for and then brought the card machine.

'Was everything all right?' she asked, as it went through.

'Fine,' I said. 'I really enjoyed it.'

'Thank you,' she said taking the note I had left as a tip on the table. I finished my drink.

'Get you another?' asked Arnold.

I could easily have said no, and for a moment had almost decided to say so, but then I changed my mind. I quite fancied staying in the pub for a while, and it was better to be in a conversation than to sit alone.

'So what is it? White wine, yes?'

'Pinot grigio.'

'One of those,' he said to the barman, 'and a pint in there.'

He brought the drinks to the table.

'Cheers.'

He grinned again, in what seemed a naturally easy-going way. He must have been about fifty, a little older than me, I'd say, with a face that looked ruddy, possibly from exposure to the wind, partly maybe to alcohol, but benign. He had been wearing a cap on when I saw him the first time. Now I could see that he had wiry grizzled hair, partly receding but over the collar at the back.

'So you're down for the weekend again.'

'Yes. I had a cancellation so I thought I'd treat myself.'

'Why not? So you've got a place here then.'

'Yes. The Nook.'

'Up by the steps?'

'You know it?'

'Yes. Used to be Christina's place.'

'Christina? Who's Christina?'

'Christina Tasse. Artist.'

'An old aunt had it for years. Not an artist though, and not a Christina.'

'No, well, Christina goes back before that. Pre-war, I mean, First War, that is. Maybe after that too. Don't really know that much. But she had a studio there. Some of them rented places just as studios, rather than to live.'

'Some of them? Some of who?'

'The Staithes Group they called it. A lot of artists came here. As I say mainly before the war.'

'Interesting,' I said. 'So I'm staying at Christina's place. Christina... what did you say?'

'Tasse.'

'Christina Tasse.' I had a momentary impulse to tell him about my odd experience of the morning of my last visit, the morning when I had first bumped into him, in fact, but it quickly passed. It was one thing confessing all to Miriam, my doctor: quite another to a complete stranger. Instead, I turned the subject to him.

'I do a bit of painting myself,' he said. 'In the summer I sell a few paintings to undiscerning tourist. I have no originality but enough technique to produce the kind of thing people go for. Small canvases. Thirty quid a shot. Stuff people can afford.'

'And you fish.'

'I fish. Mackerel. Pollock. Occasional seabass.'

'And fishfingers when the real fish don't bite.'

'Exactly. Oh and I do a bit of picture framing for people.'

'Sound like a nice life.'

'It's all right. Suits me.'

'And you get by?'

'I have a bit of a pension from the army. Not a millionaire lifestyle, but yes I get by.'

I bought a round to make it even, and we talked for another twenty minutes before I made my way back. I told him a little bit about the business, but not really anything about my personal circumstances, and he didn't push me to find out.

But I was curious about Christina Tasse. For a moment when I got back in, I'd forgotten her name, and almost went back to ask him to remind me, but then it came back. Christina Tasse. I'd certainly never heard of her, but she must have been sufficiently well known to have a name people remembered so many years later. The name sounded foreign, probably Austrian or French, but it was interesting to think that someone had once been an artist within these four walls.

You couldn't imagine it now, really, because, though I'd tried to keep some original features, it was with the aim of making it chic rather than authentic. I couldn't really remember what it was like when my ageing relative lived here, except that it was vaguely cosy and chintzy.

Christina Tasse. I decided I'd look her up when I got back home.

I had a couple more glasses of wine and then went to bed.

Sometimes when I've had a drink, I fall asleep very quickly and sleep deeply for an hour or so and then wake up and stay fully awake for about four hours, finding one thing or another to worry about. I'm told it's something to do with the metabolism when the effects of the alcohol wear off. Tonight was one of those nights – or at least seemed to be - when I suddenly woke up at about one, feeling that sleep had deserted me.

Then, quite distinctly, I heard the sound of someone moving around downstairs, not quietly or cautiously but as if carrying out a series of tasks, like tidying up, putting things away in their place, moving the furniture. And I thought I heard singing, too, a quiet sort of absent-minded humming, almost tuneless, the way children sometimes sing unconsciously when they are playing.

All this to me, in the darkness of the early hours, was much more scary than hearing the door-latch go in the light of dawn. I couldn't move. I've heard that people having nightmares sometimes feel that something, or someone, a hobgoblin or something, is sitting heavily on their chest making it impossible to move, and I've also heard that this is a mental device to prevent someone hurting themselves in the middle of a terrible dream. Whatever may be the explanation, that is how I felt, immobilised, too terrified to move. And then, to make it worse, I heard footsteps on the stair, soft footsteps noticeable more for the creaking wood they caused than for themselves. I tried to scream, but again I couldn't. There was simply nothing there, not even a muted gargle in my throat. Maybe I whimpered a little, I don't know, but what I do know is that I heard breathing in the room, and after a moment that strange little tuneless ditty, one that no-one would ever sing if they thought someone else was listening.

Next, gradually, without me being in any way aware of the reason for it, the terror lapsed away from me. The singing had stopped, but the breathing continued, very softly, almost as if the breather, whoever or whatever it was, was falling asleep; and I felt sleep coming back over me too, almost like a blanket that was being folded round me, and with it I felt a sense of well-being, a bit like the feeling I once had when my dentist gave me gas instead of the needle, almost like having marijuana.

When I woke up again, it was another bright clear morning, and I knew, immediately, that there was no other explanation for what had happened than that it was a dream. Or a partial dream, for I was sure that I had been awake for at least part of it. But the house was exactly as it should be. If, the previous time, there had been the possibility that someone had come into the house and then run off, now there was nothing.

I told myself that it was a dream, and I was reassured by this explanation. I certainly didn't feel any residual anxiety. I had a bit of breakfast and a short walk round the village, then up to the carpark. Then I packed and began to drive home.

The odd thing was, the further I drove, and the more I thought about it, the less it seemed like a dream at all.

As ever, the rigours of a workday Monday drove away any remaining idle thoughts of this nature, and I was glad of that. Normality, however dull, is sometimes necessary and welcome. Over coffee, I told Jenny about meeting Arnold. She, true to form, immediately jumped to conclusions.

'Do you fancy him, then?'

'Don't be ridiculous,' I retorted.

'What's he like? Come on, I want a complete description.'

'No.'

'Why?'

'Because if I do, you'll automatically assume I fancy him.'

'Just because you won't describe him, doesn't mean you *don't* fancy him, though. Probably the opposite.'

'Not sure I follow the logic of that.'

'I see a whirlwind holiday romance by the sea coming on,' said Jenny, in a dreamy voice.

We both laughed. It was good to have a bit of banter, even if I was the butt of the humour.

Also during that week, I began to google what I could find out about Christina Tasse. To begin with, I was pleased to find out that she was, like me, from Leeds. That she was born in 1890, died 1971. That she had been to Leeds Art School. I hadn't been to Art School, but as I've said, art and design had been one of my subjects at college, and so I felt a certain affinity with her. I, too had been an art student once upon a time; then I had been all too eager to throw it over to put myself into the capable hands of Martin, just as eager as I had been to renounce my own name and take on his.

2

Chapter 2

Christina, Staithes, 1910

What is that?' asked the young woman, pointing ahead through the carriage window. The train had left the station at Ruswarp a few moments before, on the last leg of the journey to Whitby. The man travelling in the same carriage, interrupted not for the first time by questions from his young fellow traveller, looked up from his newspaper. 'It's the Larpool viaduct,' he replied. 'It carries the railway from Scarborough to Whitby over the River Esk, which is the river you see, running alongside our own track.'

'I so wish that our line took us over it. The view must be so romantic!'

The gentleman smiled. Having been at first slightly irritated by the young woman's questions, he was now a little charmed. She was perhaps nineteen or twenty, he guessed, with what one might almost call a shock of rich dark hair, taken up rather untidily, and dark eyes. Very attractive, was his judgement, though not beautiful, perhaps; he was a man whose ideal of beauty was that of the English rose, blue-eyed and fair; but the girl had a vitality and a touch of naivety which charmed him.

'Are you travelling just to Whitby or beyond?' he asked, now folding his newspaper and putting it aside.

'Oh beyond,' she replied, with alacrity. 'To Staithes. I'm to become an artist.'

'Really?'

'Yes.' She thought for a moment, before continuing. 'Well I am an artist already, and an art student, but now I am to meet with people who are artists with pictures hung everywhere, and I believe I am to become one of them. Have you heard of an artist called Mr Charles Penner?'

The fellow traveller had to admit that he had not.

'He is my mentor, and I am to be his assistant.'

'And what does that involve?' asked the gentleman, who had heard some rum things about the bohemian lifestyle of artists.

The girl furrowed her brow for a moment; in truth she did not fully know the answer to the question. 'I will help him. To mix colours for the palette. To prepare canvases. We will converse about scenes and landscapes. I will sketch and paint under his guidance; sometimes I will model for him.'

'Model for him? How?' The gentleman had heard that modelling sometimes involved nudity.

'Just that. Sitting for him. In my college we were taught to draw from classical busts, but it's so much better to draw real life.'

'I see. And your parents. Do they approve of this?'

'Oh yes. They commissioned Mr Penner to do a portrait of me.'

'Did they indeed?'

'Have you heard the expression *en plein air*?' she asked, but before the gentleman could answer or she explain, the train was slowing down, with the associated noises of strained metal and a hissing of steam from the wheels, as it came into Whitby.

'I am at a loss as to what to do next,' she confided in the gentleman, as he made ready to descend.

'You need simply to take the shuttle from here up to Whitby Westcliff, and there join the train to Loftus which will take you to Staithes. A porter will show you. Goodbye.'

'Thank you. Goodbye.'

Twenty minutes later, she found herself on the platform of the said Whitby Westcliff station with her luggage. She gave the porter a small tip and sat down on a bench to await the train which, she had been informed, would be arriving in ten minutes.

Reflecting on the earlier stages of her journey, Leeds to York, York to Pickering, Pickering to Whitby, she was pleased to have had the chance to announce herself as an artist. It was a beginning, and perhaps all beginnings were small; it had given her a little practice at saying who she was.

This person she was becoming.

An artist.

To be perfectly honest, she had not enjoyed her first term at the College of Art in Leeds.

At Miss Henderson's little school in Headingly, which rather grandiosely she had called an *Academy for Young Ladies*, her natural skill with the pencil had attracted favourable comment, and it had been her father's idea that, at the age of fourteen, she should begin to attend the college. He was himself a man of business, a manufacturer of machinery for industrial purposes, but he was a lover and patron of the arts, especially painting and music, and he numbered amongst his acquaintances, practitioners and curators in those fields.

Whereas Miss Henderson's Academy had been small and cosy, however, the rooms and corridors of the College were gloomy and seemed to echo with unfriendliness, it seemed to her at first. The female students were generally scoffed at by the young men. They were excluded from certain classes, especially life study. Females were not allowed to see other living female bodies, even when draped, for fear that some fundamental precept of decency would be broken and their maidenly innocence somehow tarnished. Instead, as she had said to the gentleman on the train, they were ushered into different rooms where they were permitted to draw from classical busts and statues.

It was with the appearance of Mr Penner, not a regular teacher at the college but an occasional visiting tutor, that she had begun to understand the difference between being good at drawing and having a passion for art. Mr Penner told them of the Impressionists and demonstrated some of the techniques of brushwork and style he had learned from visiting galleries and studios in Paris and Amsterdam. It was a new way of looking at the world, he said. Not naturalism, but closer to truth than naturalism because it does not merely copy the surface of nature but analyses its components minutely and finds new ways of expressing it. It is not just learning how to paint, but how to see.

It was also Mr Penner who had introduced to the students the practice of painting *en plein air* rather than in a studio, and on numerous occasions she had persuaded her family to take picnics, to Becketts Park, to Kirkstall Abbey, to Meanwood, where she would set up her easel, or sit with her pad on her knee.

'Christina's work is extraordinarily promising, Mr Tasse,' Mr Penner had said to her father at a meeting to set up an art fund for the City Art Gallery. Her success had made her father even more of an enthusiast.

And if she had been flattered to hear that, how much more pleased had she been, a year later, when he had spoken to her father again, expressing his wish to take her on as an assistant, a kind of apprentice.

The prospect had filled her with an enthusiasm she had never known before, and now it was happening. For days her excitement had been bubbling.

Now, as she sat on the platform of Whitby Westcliff, she was calmer. She did not want to appear, on her arrival at Staithes, as a giddy girl!

Her mother, ever nervous, had not wanted her to undertake this journey alone. Her father, always a robust champion of her independence had taken the other view. 'Mr Penner will be there to meet her in Staithes. I will take her to the station in Leeds. I'm sure she has been brought up to be quite capable of negotiating a couple of platform changes on the way.'

There was a low throaty cough from the engine's chimney, and then another, and then, like an old man, grown stiff with rest, easing himself painfully into motion, the train drew forward. Through the dwellings of the outskirts, they went, and then into open pasture with the wide expanse of the sea to their right, and shortly over a viaduct, much smaller than the one she had seen before Whitby and constructed from metal girders. A minute later, another viaduct took them across a little valley with a village below and immediately afterwards they pulled into a station, whose sign announced itself as Sandsend.

Hearing the clatter of doors, she watched as a mother with two children left the train, then a clergyman; further down another family with a nurse, and three or four men, striding briskly; then came the guard's shrill whistle, and once more, with gruff complaint, the engine edged forward, amidst a creaking and groaning of its wheels.

They drew away from the station building and the sea became visible again below. The track wound along a curving shelf above the cliffs, giving sudden changes of aspect; at each moment Christina could see the potential of a different painting: rocks, stacks, trees, sea; it was all very thrilling. No wonder, she thought, that so many artists loved to come to this part of Yorkshire to find subjects for their paintings.

The track now came into a steep-sided cutting and a moment later, with a buffet of air, entered a tunnel. A dim gas lamp was the only light in the carriage, all the sounds now became muffled, and smoke and steam surged along past the windows. Though the windows were closed, a faint soft smell of damp smoke seeped into the carriage. Then, after perhaps a half a minute, daylight came suddenly back; the sea was visible again, and billows of white smoke flattened over a meadow beside the track.

How many colours was the sea made up of, she pondered as she looked away towards the horizon. And what looked like blue, was that really blue or a combination of other colours and impressions? And then the sky – the sky with its ever-changing cloud combinations – how could you represent the sky truthfully? Another wide bay came into view, with a village at its head; the track swept inland and a few minutes later the train slowed and came into the station at Kettleness. Hinderwell was only a short distance further. A brief stop at each. And then, Staithes, where, with a new shiver of excitement, she waited for the train to stop and then descended to the platform.

3

Chapter 3

Christina, letters from Staithes, 1910

From Christina Tasse to Mr & Mrs A Tasse 7ᵗʰ April

Dear father and mother

I arrived last night, safely, and Mr Penner met me at the station in Staithes and brought me here to the house in Roxby, two miles inland from the village. My trunk, I was glad to find, had arrived the previous day. I have only met Mrs Penner once before. She is very pleasant and welcoming, but does not, I sense, take a great interest in Mr Penner's work.

The house here is a rather sprawling farmhouse which Mr Penner rents for the entire summer, for himself and his family. My room is in the attic, looking out over fields, and it is spacious and comfortable. Mr and Mrs Penner have their own separate rooms in one wing of the house, and the children are in the other. Downstairs there is a large reception room, a playroom for the children, a large kitchen, a dining room, a smaller sitting room which Mrs Penner sometimes uses, and the maid's and cook's quarters, to the rear. There are some outhouses which, Mr Penner tells me are useful for the storage of materials, though most of our painting will be done outdoors.

Mr Rutter was here when I arrived. He knows you, father, he tells me, from meetings in Leeds, so you will know that he is a great proponent of impressionism and modernism in art, and he speaks quite passionately about the sad reluctance of the art establishment, as he calls it, to feature the work of living artists.

We had dinner and sat talking until about nine o'clock, Mrs Penner having retired some time earlier. I wondered if Mr Rutter was a guest at the house, or just a day visitor, but feeling tired, I made my own excuses at last and left the two men deep in conversation. I had rather hoped, on my first evening, to speak to Mr Penner about my work and duties, but it was interesting nonetheless to hear the strong views of so important a man as Mr Rutter.

I am writing this before breakfast as I woke early, feeling refreshed from my journey after a good night's sleep, and knowing you will be pleased to hear from

Your loving daughter
Christina

From Christina Tasse to Millicent Houghton, Leeds, 23rd April

My dearest Milly

You asked me to report on my adventures here, so, now that I am settled, this is my first instalment.

The landscape in these parts has in every way lived up to my expectations. It has some of the wildness of our moors, but little of their bleakness. In addition there is the sea and I fear words will fail me in describing the grandeur and beauty of the coastal features. The villages along the coast, often tightly locked in between beetling cliffs, rocky ravines, and river estuaries, are, in themselves, greatly picturesque, though the lives of their inhabitants, mainly fisher folk, are very hard.

At first I was somewhat intimidated by the locals. They are down-to-earth plain spoken people and I feared they would regard me, a young woman with what to them must seem a leisurely and privileged existence, as a dilettante. However, their bark, as you might say, is worse than their bite, and you don't have to search very deeply before you find qualities of warmth and hospitality. There is also, as Mr Penner told me, and as I have found myself, a fund of goodwill between the natives and the artistic community.

I was a little disappointed to find that the artistic community is smaller than it once was at about the turn of the century. Quite a number of the former denizens have upped sticks and moved to such places as Newlyn Bay and Lamorna in Cornwall, where the weather, they say, is more clement than here, and where there is quite a colony of English painters who mix freely with visitors from the continent. Mr Penner says my education will not be complete until I have visited the centres abroad, in France and Belgium particularly, where the new ideas flourish, in order to talk to and study the work of painters there, but for the moment at least I am more than happy to remain here at Staithes to make the most of the opportunities it affords.

Please remember me to your mother and father. I look forward to hearing from you and in particular to how you are finding the profession of teaching.

Until then, I remain your affectionate friend,
Christina

From Christina Tasse to Mr A Tasse 6th May
Dear Father
Please thank Henry for his letter. I know he is at an age when sitting down to write to an elder sister may not be a preferred way of passing time, so it was especially nice to hear from him. He told me – I'm sure in all seriousness – that I needn't reply, as you keep him fully informed

by reading my letters aloud. I shall abide by his wishes, but please convey how much I miss him.

I had a slight cold earlier in the week but I have now recovered completely. I walked along the cliff path from Staithes to Port Mulgrave yesterday and I am sure the brisk wind blew away any lingering germs! Whilst in Staithes, I looked at some of the cottages which have occasionally been rented out, in part or wholly, as studios.

I have discussed with Mr Penner the possibility of taking on such a studio for myself at some point in the next couple of months. He is not entirely against the idea, but feels that it is perhaps too soon yet, and, despite my enthusiasm, I know that he is right. However, His opinion is that it is something to be considered as I begin to find my feet as an independent artist.

Thank you for setting up the arrangement with the bank in Whitby. I paid a visit last week and confirmed that everything is in order. My expenses are slight, and as you know Mr Penner refuses point blank to take anything for my keep, but it is convenient to have access to some funds and I was able to profit from my visit to the town to buy some small necessary things for myself.

You will be pleased to know that Mr Penner's portrait, the one of me, I mean, has been started. I have decided to wear the white dress which mother gave me as a Christmas present. As yet Mr Penner has only completed preliminary sketches, as he likes to spend as much time working in the open air as he possibly can, as do I, and I much prefer painting to being a subject, but I will keep you updated of the progress.

Give my regards to cook, to Ethel and to Catherine. I hope they are all well.

Your devoted daughter
Christina

From Christina Tasse to Millicent Houghton, Leeds, May 12th

Dearest Milly

I am sorry to hear that your chest complaint has kept you confined for so many weeks. I am sure that the rigours of the classroom are not always conducive to the best of health! I hope, now that the warmer season approaches, that your recovery and convalescence will be swift.

Today, we have had unbroken rain so far, and James, the gardener, assures us that it will last for the rest of the day. Happily, this has provided me with a little extra leisure time which I will devote to bringing you up to date with my progress.

I will remain, for the moment, with the subject of the weather. We have had, during the Spring, some tremendous gales and storms. The sea, in these conditions, is an awesome sight, never more so than when it crashes against the cliffs and outlying rocks. In Staithes, where the village stands at the head of a rocky cove, it is dangerous to walk near the harbour when these monstrous seas approach as they are often known to surge into the lower parts of the village itself. Also at Staithes, there is a huge viaduct, carrying the railway across the river gorge, and for several days in April, it was considered unsafe for trains to venture across, so high was the gale.

It is no exaggeration to say that a very fine line marks the difference between life and death for the villagers here. Every time a boat leaves the harbour there is no certainty that it will return unscathed, and the people live with a kind of fatalism in their hearts. Mr Penner tells me that there have been numerous tragedies during the years he has been coming here. I pray every night that none will happen to which I must have to bear witness.

As mentioned, I am somewhat confined by the weather today. Not so Mr Penner. The doctrine of painting en plein air is one he adheres to rigorously, and at times it entails a heroic determination to brave the elements whatever they may be. I like to think of myself as a proponent of this school, but I do not complain when I am excused on account of the severity of the weather.

You asked me in an earlier letter to describe Mr Penner and his family to you. I fear I have signally failed to do so as yet, so I will attempt it now. Charles Penner is in his thirties, I would say, perhaps late thirties. His wife, Mary is possibly a little older, though I am only guessing on outward appearances, and I may be quite erroneous. They have three children, Anne who is eleven, James who is eight, and Melissa who is six, but who will be seven in a few weeks' time. They spend the summer months here and the children attend the local school; in the winter, they return to Bradford, though Charles Penner sometimes comes here alone if his subject is a winter landscape. Mrs Penner is small woman, slightly plump and with a pleasant face. She is very attentive to the children and is patient with her husband with regard to his artistic comings and go-ings, which do not always follow the orderly pattern of family life. Mr Penner is not exactly tall, but above average height for a man, I would say, with dark hair and sideburns and with blue eyes that are kindly but which can also be piercing.

I feel that I am learning a great deal here, but I can honestly say that I have not yet produced a single work of any true merit. Mr Penner gives me regular criticisms as I work, and this I welcome as without it I fear that I will never progress. There is a danger that I am aware of, and that he too has drawn attention to, that my work has come to resemble his in certain aspects of technique, but this I see as being not entirely a neg-ative thing. I know that I am very young, and that my apprenticeship must go through numerous stages before I find my true artistic self, and [though you might not always remember me as such] I am very patient!

You may be interested to know, by the way, that I spent a day in Whitby recently. It is only a short journey by train from here, and I was accompanied by Harriet, who is the daughter of the curate and a lit-tle older than myself. It is a very picturesque town, situated around the estuary of prettily named River Esk, and surrounded on each side by very steep hills which greatly add to the charm. Harriet was very keen to point out to me the ruined abbey which stands on a very high eminence above the town and which has a very romantic aspect. It is one of the locations, Harriet informed me, in Mr Stoker's novel of Dracula which she has read. She led me up the hundred and ninety-nine steps to the church and the abbey, in the footsteps of several of the novel's protagonists, it seems, and even showed me a gravestone to which Mr Stoker explicitly referred. It is a dark tale, full of horrors, and our talk all the way home was of nothing but vampires. I have no doubt that vampires exist only in the imagination, but nevertheless the very thought makes one shiver!

Write to me soon, dear Milly, and take great care of yourself.
Christina

From Christina Tasse to Millicent Houghton, Leeds, June 10th
Dear Milly
I am glad to hear that you are now returned from Switzerland, and that your stay there has had a beneficial effect on your health. I spent some time at home in Leeds at the end of the month, and was looking forward to seeing you, but alas it was not to be.

My family are well, thank you. Henry was away at school, of course, so unfortunately, I missed him too. Mother complains that without us both there the house seems empty, and extracted a promise that I would return more frequently, and I shall try to keep to my word. I feel sorry for her, for father leads a very busy social life as well as work, and she is on her own somewhat, but it is difficult to explain to her how absorbing my life as, dare I say it, an artist, has become.

It is very kind of you to say that you would like a painting of mine to hang in your bedroom, and as soon as I have one ready, I shall make a gift of it to you. There is a particular scene which I have in mind for such a painting, and I shall start on it soon.

I think I mentioned to you that Mr Penner had been commissioned by my parents to paint a portrait of me, and I shall tell you of an incident which happened recently that has left quite an impression on me. Progress on the portrait has been intermittent [Mr Penner has made no secret of the fact that portrait painting is not his favourite form] but last week we were bound by the sea-fog for two days, and so there was nothing for it but to work indoors. I fear I am not the best of 'sitters' – I tend to fidget and my mind runs on impatiently to what I am planning to do next, but in my effort to stay still, I was able to watch Mr Penner closely, and to see the intense concentration he brings to his work. I have noticed this when seeing him at work outdoors, and it is no wonder that he tires himself, but the relationship of artist and sitter is one which brings a very private kind of awareness. As I say, I am a bit of a fidgeter, and occasionally he came to correct me, adjusting my position and pose. At one point, he tipped my chin, seemed to study me closely, and there was such a prolonged engagement of our eyes that I felt a very strange nervous excitement, something I have never felt before or ever expected. After a moment, he returned to his place, but as if his concentration had been broken entirely, he soon brought the session to an end. I sensed that he was disturbed or upset and for the next two days, he seemed to avoid me completely. At last, I summoned the courage to ask, have I done something wrong, have I offended you in some way? No, he replied, squeezing his eyes tight shut for a moment and then opening them and smiling, nothing, he said, taking my hand and patting it affectionately, nothing at all.

I am sure that even in telling you this I am exaggerating its importance, and I will not be surprised or offended if you tell me I am being ridiculous, but as I have said, it made an impression on me, and I am sometimes helpless to prevent my butterfly mind from returning to dwell on it. Perhaps my imagination has been too much engaged in thinking of vampires and the like, but I am sure Mr Penner is no Dracula!

But the length of this letter shows how shamefully self-absorbed I have become! Please tell me more of your impressions of Switzerland, a country about which I have heard so much, and one which I would love to visit. Perhaps some day, you and I will go there together on a tour. How marvellous that would be!

Please write again soon. I shall be eagerly awaiting your next letter.
Christina

From Christina Tasse to Millicent Houghton, Leeds, August
Dear Milly

I am so pleased to hear of your good news. I hardly know Mr Thorpe but from your description he seems to be a perfectly pleasant and agreeable gentleman, and I am sure he will regard you as something of a catch, as they say! You must be feeling very happy and I am sure you will enjoy all the delectable little preparations that will lead up to a June wedding next year. Has it been decided yet where you will go on honeymoon? I expect it will be Venice or Rome or some other such romantic place.

I don't recall if I mentioned it earlier, but for my part I will be travelling in the second half of the summer, or probably September to France and to Belgium. It is being planned by Mr Penner and though it is a trip essentially for educational purposes, I am feeling very excited about it.

In the meantime, I have taken on, temporarily, a small studio in Staithes and spend some time there several days a week, staying overnight on some occasions. It is a cottage, tiny by any standard, but with a small living space downstairs, a rather primitive stove, and water from a tap outside. Up a rickety staircase, is a room with a bolster, lumpy but adequate. I tend to work up here as there is a better quality of light than downstairs. The bathroom arrangements are, to say the least, primitive, but I make do!

It gives me a little taste of independence and freedom, and it is good to have my own space, one in which to impose my own disciplines of work. Mother was very apprehensive when I told her, but I was able, with father's support, to reassure her. This place contains no threats other than the occasionally wild weather, and besides, Mr Penner calls regularly to keep an eye on me.

During the day, I wander with my box of tricks and easel, identifying subjects for future paintings and sketching like mad.

I am a poor housekeeper, however. Yesterday, I forgot that I had run out of oil and candles, and had to sit in darkness for an hour before going to bed, as it was too late to return to Roxby!

As soon as I know the exact dates of my travel, I shall let you know. I am certain to be calling in at Leeds and staying for a few days both before and afterwards, and I am sure we will be able to arrange to meet. It has been too long!

Your dear friend, Christina

From Christina Tasse to Mr A Tasse, August 10th
Dear father,

I am writing now to confirm the date for our ferry crossing to Belgium. It is 6th September, and I will need to depart from Leeds no later than seven o'clock in the morning to be at Hull for the crossing.

I plan to return home by the end of August, so there will be plenty of time to make arrangements. Please reassure mother. I know she bothers her head about me but there is absolutely no need. I am an independent young woman, and I am quite capable of looking after myself.

By the way, the portrait of myself is now complete, and Mr Penner says he will deliver it in person before we leave for the continent.

I do hope Henry will still be at home when I return. When does his school term begin? Tell him I shall take him to the gallery and treat him to tea and buns up in town.

I am so looking forward to seeing you all again,

Your devoted daughter, Christina

4

Chapter 4

Anna, Staithes, 2010

Whether I intended it or not, it was difficult to avoid bumping into Arnold at some point during the day, whenever I was in Staithes. And I went there three or four times over the next couple of months. Once, he offered to take me out in his boat, but I told him I wasn't ready for that yet, probably never! His place was just a little way along and set back from the road, a pretty typical old fisherman's cottage, though inside it looked more like a studio than a residence, with frames, both empty and full, scattered everywhere, along with other paraphernalia of the trade, tools and materials for framing – oh, and some of his fishing gear too. He didn't entertain often, he explained, with a wry smile, by way of excusing the disorder. But I enjoyed my conversations with him. Despite his unconventional way of life there was something sane and trustworthy about him.

The season was changing. Though some days were still bitterly cold and wet, there were one or two pleasantly mild days, and it was even possible to sit outside at the pub at times. That is where we usually met and chatted, either inside or out, and the topic we talked about most was Christina.

I should say that I had had no further strange encounters but because I now linked the house with her, I had become curious. Of course,

I didn't tell Arnold directly about any of this, but it was easy enough to turn the conversation round, and I think he found it as convivial a topic as I did.

As I have said, I had begun to do a little bit of research in the evenings. I am not at all the sort of person who goes in for building family trees and that sort of genealogical stuff, but I did go on the government census website and found out a few things.

She was born in 1890, the daughter of Arthur and Caroline Tasse. The census of 1901 shows that they were living in Far Headingly, and that they had a cook, a maidservant, and a nurse – so obviously a reasonably prosperous family. There was a younger brother, Henry, born 1897. Father was a businessman dealing in machine tools, of French extraction, her mother originally from Ireland. In 1905, she began to attend the Art College at Leeds. At some point, she came into contact with Charles Penner, an artist living in Bradford, who had connections in Leeds, and who was a member of the Staithes group. She became his assistant, and 'a close friendship developed between them'. She accompanied him on trips to Bruges, Amsterdam, and Paris. A portrait of her by him, was commissioned by her parents when she was twenty. Apart from this there was little biographical information about her. There were references to some of her paintings, by galleries and Art Dealers, but the blurb about her was minimal.

I fed all this, over a couple of drinks, to Arnold, who nodded his head with interest. It was mostly new to him, though he recognised the name of Charles Penner straight away.

'A lot of the others went down to Cornwall. He stayed here. True Yorkshireman! Had a house built over in Sandsend. Not a household name, but definitely mentioned in the Art books.'

'What do you think about this, though, that, you know, a close friendship etc and then she accompanied him to Bruges?'

'You mean, did they have an affair?'

'Well, what do you think?'

He shrugged his shoulders. 'From what you've said, he would have been quite a bit older than her.'

'Yes.'

'Married with three children.'

'Perhaps she turned his head.'

'Stranger things have been known.'

'Young women do fall in love with older men...,' I mused. 'Especially talented successful men who open doorways.'

'Are you speaking from experience?'

'No,' I said returning his question with a definite laugh. I thought for a moment and then, with that odd sense of confiding in a stranger, gave him my background, or as much of it as I chose to reveal. 'I met Martin when I was seventeen and he twenty-one. I was married by twenty. I didn't have time to fantasize about older men,' I said, though it probably wasn't true. 'How about you?'

'I was married when I went in the army. Couldn't hack it when I came back. She left. Not her fault. I was difficult to live with. Drank too much.'

'Kids?'

'Couple of girls.'

'Do you ever see them?'

'No.'

He didn't elaborate. I didn't push it. He had chosen the life of a loner, as I suppose I was doing, in my own way. It wasn't for me to question him. I wondered if he ever had affairs. Perhaps when the summer season brought the tourists in, there might be the possibility of encounters, but again I didn't question him. I didn't feel I could go there.

'Are you painting anything at the moment?' I asked, changing the subject.

'A few things. Some near copies.'

'What are near copies?'

'Existing paintings. Not too famous, obviously. But the kind of thing people like.'

'You don't paint in plein air, then?' I asked, borrowing a phrase I had come across reading about Christina.

He gave one of his little self-deprecating laughs. 'And catch pneumonia? There was a reason a lot of them went down to Cornwall.'

'You can always layer up.'

'Sometimes, in the summer, if the mood takes me. Always seems a lot of canvas to fill when it's all your own work. And then tourists like to stand and watch. Prefer the studio on the whole.'

'I read somewhere that the villagers used to model for them, in the old days, I mean.'

'Yes, I've heard that, too. A farthing a go. Mind you, a farthing was probably worth quite a bit in those days.'

'They didn't mind them, then?'

'How do you mean?'

'Well, droves of artists descending on them.'

'Apparently not. Well, I suppose if they brought money...'

'And a bit of colour. I guess life would have been pretty bleak.'

'Do you want to know what they did object to? The villagers...'

'Go on,' I said, wondering if he was going to reveal some dark secrets of bohemian moral turpitude.

'Painting on Sundays. The Sabbath.'

'Really?'

'Work, you see. Well, you must have noticed all the chapels here.'

I had, though I had also concluded that most of them were holiday lets these days.

'Wesleyans. Primitive Methodists. Very religious. Superstitious. People who make their living from the sea are always superstitious. Were, anyway.'

I looked up at the photographs on the wall again, especially the dramatic ones which captured the storm waves, and tried to imagine the arduous and dangerous lives those inhabitants must have had.

'For those in peril on the sea,' said Arnold, reading my mind, though when I looked at him, he was grinning. 'Another drink?'

'No,' I replied. 'Got to drive back tomorrow. Need a clear head!'

Though in fact, when I got back in, I did pour myself a glass of wine and sat for a time. I was half wondering, as I did most nights, if I might get another visitation in the morning.

I was awake early, and I listened. For about half an hour, it must have been, and then I drifted off to sleep again. Then, opening my eyes, I fancied I had just heard the click of the latch. I threw the bedclothes off and scurried downstairs. The kitchen door was closed, and the bolt locked. Even so, and I guess feeling disappointed, I opened the door and peeked down the alley. There was nothing. Either my Christina ghost was getting fainter, or, as I really suspected, the whole thing was in my imagination.

5

Chapter 5

A crowded café, with a view over the River Reie. Outside, a street performer with a mandolin. Inside, the clatter of glasses and cups, and a din of feverish chatter; the air thick with the smoke of pipes and cheroots. Her companion Charles Penner is talking, half in French, half in German to Friedrich, an Austrian sculptor. She has lost track of the conversation.

They have been in Bruges for four days. And before that, three days in Amsterdam. And each day has been like this, scurrying from one atelier to another, from one gallery here to another there, and from one café to another, meeting people, artists, either planned or by chance. It is exciting but also bemusing, as if she can never quite move fast enough to keep up with the pace.

She is disappointed with her French. She had imagined her school French to be sufficient but in fact it was far from it. She can ask for 'du café' or for 'un pain avec un peu de confiture' in the quietness of a polite breakfast parlour, but in the cut-and-thrust of real conversation it is hopeless. Especially here, in this café of artists, as Charles has called it. She feels like a fish out of water.

Opposite, at the next table, a young man with a thin straw-coloured goatee and pale blue eyes has been staring at her intently for quarter of an hour. His clothes are shabby, and his face is drawn, as if from illness or lack of nourishment. He has a rag of a handkerchief closed in his fist, and he twists the end of it between finger and thumb. She looks away, trying to ignore him. She looks out of the window towards the river, but whenever she lets her eye travel back inside, she is aware of his glance again, fixing her with solemn intentness. It is very disconcerting.

She leans towards her companion and asks quietly, 'Why is that man staring at me?'

'Perhaps he wants to paint you.'

'Who is he?'

'I have no idea. Do you want me to have a word with him?'

'No, it's all right,' she replies, not wanting to make a scene or cause embarrassment.

She takes a sip from the glass of thé à la menthe, which is now cold. Charles is drinking red wine from a bottle which he is sharing with Friedrich; almost everyone in the room seems to be drinking something stronger than tea - beer, wine, absinthe.

A woman has now come to sit beside the staring man. She is young, perhaps seventeen, thin-faced and plain but with fleshy lips and sensual eyes. She is wearing a pale chemise open at the neck, almost to her bosom. She takes a drink from his glass and then nuzzles against him, her hand on his thigh. The man pays no attention to her but continues to stare.

She is glad when the conversation between Charles and Friedrich ends, and they prepare to leave. Friedrich is effusive in his leave taking; he hugs Charles and pats his shoulder vigorously; he takes both of her hands in his and kisses them, saying 'au revoir, a la prochaine fois, m'selle.'

As they walk along the riverside there is a smell of chestnuts and wood smoke; evening is drawing on. A man with an accordion plays beneath a gas lamp and a child holds out a hat. Mr Penner throws in a little change and the child makes a practised bow.

They call in at a chophouse for their meal. She tries a little wine, but the taste is strong and sour, and she doesn't quite like it, though the effect makes her more relaxed. Then they return to the small pension where they have been staying. Mr Penner asks her if she wishes to go out again later, but she says no, she is a little tired, she will go to bed early. He asks if she minds if he goes out, and she says, no, of course not. A little later, from the window of her room, which overlooks the street, she sees him going out.

She draws a chair up to the window and watches life outside. It is a small side street so not much is going on; occasionally a couple pass by arm in arm, sometimes a group of men, going off to drink, she supposes. On the corner, a woman is waiting, and she wonders if she is a prostitute; before coming here, she had hardly known what a prostitute was, she had certainly never seen one, at least to her knowledge. Here, no-one seems to think it strange or bad to see prostitutes on the street. Some of them, Mr Penner had explained, are models who earn extra money this way, or who are no longer wanted as sitters for anyone. Or dancers who have outgrown their art and fallen on hard times.

It is all quite bewildering.

She has wavered between excitement and confusion, exhilaration and frustration. Sometimes she has wakened in the morning with a renewed energy and appetite for what new experiences the day will have to offer her; usually by the late afternoon, if not sooner, her spirits have become depressed.

It is all a far cry from the peaceful and predictable world of Staithes.

The next day, they set out for Paris, and she is genuinely excited at the prospect of seeing a city she has heard so much about and which has such romantic associations. The trains are less comfortable than those in England. They are in one of the better compartments but even so the benches are hard, especially to sit on for any length of time. And at the stations where they stop, no-one seems to have thought of the obvious needs of a lady on a lengthy journey, whereas the men, evidently, are able simply to take care of themselves! Nevertheless, she watches the rolling hills and open countryside of Picardy, with its neat coppices and pretty rivers, and is determined to enjoy the journey.

They stay for two nights on the outskirts of Paris, with Armand, an old friend of Charles, and his wife, Annette. Armand, who is a sculptor and engraver, is a giant of a fellow, with a full dark beard, big features, and a hearty laugh; Annette, younger than him by quite a few years, as she guesses, is small and lithe in her movements, as if she could be a dancer. She has beautiful, beguiling eyes, like a lynx, but with a hint of both mirth and slyness.

In the evening, Charles and Armand go off to the tavern together; she talks to Annette and tries to practise her French. Annette is patient and speaks slowly so that she can follow. It is pleasing and she thinks she is making progress, though it will be a long time before she will have the capacity to speak of art and its broader issues. Annette tells her a little about herself. She is from Rouen, where Armand had a studio. I was his model, she says, then his mistress; and then, when his wife died, I took over from her!

They both laugh.

When Armand and Charles return, they open a bottle of red wine and all four have a glass. It is sweeter than the wine she had in Bruges, but heavier and, she thinks, probably stronger. It makes her feel drowsy.

When she wakes in the early morning, the peacefulness of the dawn chorus is broken, after a time, by sounds which, as they grow louder, she identifies as those of Armand and Annette making love. She is terribly embarrassed and puts her hands over her ears, but the noise elevates to a sudden awful persistent racket; it goes on for a full half minute, and then, quite suddenly stops, leaving the dawn chorus to resume.

'I hope you slept well,' says Annette at breakfast.

'Yes, very well,' she replies, trying to let the moment pass without eye contact.

The house was in a pleasant position, with a garden of herbs and vegetables and beyond that vines which were now burgeoning with fruit.

After breakfast, she sketches in the quiet of the garden.

She tries to sketch, from memory, the young man in the cafe who had stared at her so intently - his pale drawn features, his thin straggly beard, his finger and thumb playing with the corner of the handkerchief; and then the girl who came to sit beside him. And strangely, it is the girl who occupies her concentration more. The man remains a hastily sketched outline, something maybe to return to. But the girl, with her carelessly open chemise, her fleshy mouth, her obviously sensual eyes, preoccupies her more. She seems vulnerable and yet self-confident, in a way which is both fascinating and repellent. She works for an hour to capture that peculiar feeling of perhaps decadent allure. Then she puts the sketch away, showing it to no-one, not even to Charles.

That evening, their last, they sit round the table, and all speak English, in which Annette is proficient, and Armand fluent.

'I studied for a time at the Slade,' he explains. '...is where I first met Charles, yes? '

'Indeed.'

'So, Miss Tasse, have you achieved your aim of learning what is occurring at the frontiers of art.'

'I've learned a great deal,' she says, knowing that she would hardly know what to say if he asked her to qualify that remark.

'Of course, Charles he is a very good teacher. A man who understands. And can communicate. This is the great thing.'

Setting off the following morning, they cross Paris in an open cab, taking in Notre Dame, the Champs Elysees and the Louvre, the Arc de Triomphe and the Eiffel Tower, magnificent in itself, but whose merit, Charles Penner tells her, is much disputed. Then turning towards the rising slopes of Montmartre, they find lodgings on the Rue Garreau, half a mile from the church of Sacre Coeur.

The mornings they spend wandering round the galleries at the Musee de Luxembourg and the Petit Palace, and they have lunch, one day, at the Moulin de la Galette, which Charles Penner tells her, was famously painted by Renoir.

After the relative calm and tranquillity of Fresnes, they encounter once again, in Montmartre, the full hectic tumult of an artistic quarter.

She enjoys the vivid pageant of street-life, the dancers and musicians, the jugglers; the feeling that life is a never-ending carnival of the colourful and the grotesque. In the salons and cafes, and the galleries and halls, the shabby cafes and shadowy bars smelling of cabbage soup and stale red wine, they meet artists and poets, some extravagant in manner, courting fame, some self-deprecating and mournful, giving themselves up to the prospect of penury, disease and starvation. And again, she begins to feel lost.

In one café, a sculptor named Jerome, who speaks a kind of English laced with French or German phrases when his vocabulary fails, expounds his art to her, and says she must come to his studio to properly understand, but underneath the table he places his hand firmly on her knee, and she is only rescued when Charles sees her predicament. Others, when she talks to them, talk only of their own art, showing little interest in hers. And often, they argue passionately, clashing theories of nature, and realism and truth, pronouncing and denouncing, and laughing uproariously or cursing and blaspheming so that you might think that fisticuffs is about to break out.

'Don't be put off,' Mr Penner says, 'many of them are pure charlatans.' But it all makes her feel invisible, and her own claim to be an artist, nurtured in the landscape charm of remote Staithes, seems utterly flimsy.

Her companion, however, seems in his element, completely at home. As in Bruges, he sometimes goes out alone, later at night, and she supposes that the life at night-time is even more raucous and outlandish. Does he go to the music halls, she wonders, where, they say, the girls dance half-naked, and where prostitutes ply their trade. Or to other venues where the bohemian life flourishes in its night-time glory. It is both shocking and fascinating.

When left alone, she returns to the sketch of the girl, and to another version of it which she has started. It no longer bears any resemblance to the actual memory. It has become instead an image of her own creation, the mouth lascivious, the eyes devious, the chemise now open to reveal her breasts in its shadows. She realises that it represents all the sides of herself which she dare not show the world, the sides which she hardly knows herself.

On this particular evening, she takes up the sketch again. The youth has now disappeared completely, and in his place, she now begins, very patiently, to sketch the figure of Charles Penner.

An amusing evening, thought Charles Penner to himself, walking back from The Lapin Agile to the pension at the Rue Garreau. By the light of a flickering gas-lamp he checked his fob-watch and confirmed that it was nearly one o'clock in the morning. Later than he intended. He felt mildly tipsy but the cut and thrust of discussion and argument had offset the effects of drink.

Those fellows! They would probably go on until dawn! They were highly entertaining but eccentric to say the least. Especially that chap Georges and his Spanish crony, Pablo, together with Max Jacob, the witty genial friend who assists with translation.

Modernists they called themselves, futurists, revolutionaries. It had started with a discussion of the art of photography and how it might or might not influence fine arts. Naturalism exists no longer, they said. And the plein air movement is history, romanticism's last hurrah! 'Of course, no-one is saying you shouldn't go outside to paint if you feel like it but as a concept in itself, it means nothing.'

Of course, it was all good natured. The Spaniard had taken a serviette and drawn a sketch with a stick of crayon he had in his pocket. 'There, mon ami,' he had said, handing the serviette to him, 'there is your portrait.' The sketch was like a caricature made up of spare parts and fragments. They had all laughed heartily but he knew that underneath it was not intended as a joke.

It was a pity in a way that Christina hadn't been there tonight, and the thought of it made him feel slightly guilty. There had been some nights when he had been glad to get away, alone, to meet people without the constraint of being, as it were, a chaperone to his young companion. In the latter part of the trip she often seemed troubled, a little moody and uncommunicative, as if she was struggling with something. Perhaps it was all a little too much to take in, with all the travelling, too. He adored her as much as if she were his own child, but he would be glad now to get her home, to be rid of the responsibility. He would keep the serviette to show her, however, and would explain the context in which it had been drawn.

He continued his walk. It was still warm, and on the streets, plenty was going on. People were sitting outside cafes, drinking and talking, and occasionally you got a strong smell of incense or hashish or some other concoction that was being smoked. From deep inside one café, as he passed, came the sound of slightly out of tune guitar and raucous singing.

He reached the Rue Garreau at last, and mounting the stairs to the top floor, saw, from the strip of light under her door, that Christina had not yet retired. He tapped lightly on the door and waited. A moment later, the door opened, and her face appeared.

'I saw the light under your door,' he explained. 'But you are in your robe, I see. I just wanted to check that all is well. I will see you in the morning.'

'I wasn't intending to go to bed yet. Come in for a moment,' she said, opening the door for him. 'Sit down.'

'I'll just stay for a moment,' he said. 'What have you been doing. Sketching?'

'A little.'

'May I see?'

'It's nothing. There's nothing to show you.'

'Here, look at this,' he said, remembering the serviette and taking it from his pocket. 'A young Spaniard named Pablo Picasso drew it for me.'

'What is it?'

'Me apparently. What do you make of it?'

'I don't understand it.'

'No, neither do I, really, but there we are.'

'It is sometimes so confusing,' she said, looking at the at the serviette with a baffled expression.

'They agree that Cezanne is their 'master' but they also talk of primitive art. African sculptures and the like.'

'I hardly know which way to turn next.'

'Don't worry. Just trust your intuition,' he replied.

'I wish you had taken me with you tonight,' she said, after a moment. 'I thought...'

'That I was tired, yes. I was. But being alone here...'

'I'm sorry. I have been remiss,' he said. 'I should not have left you to your own devices quite so much.'

'I just feel that I don't fit in. The more I see, the less I understand, and the less I feel like an artist than a prim schoolgirl.'

'My dear!' he said, standing as he saw tears starting in her eyes, and offering his hands in a gesture of comfort.

'I can't learn about art until I learn about life,' she pleads, her voice full of emotion.

'There, there,' he said as she came into his arms like a child. 'Tomorrow night we will go out together, like free spirits, and we will get drunk and stay out until three in the morning, how is that?'

The sob in her voice mixed with an involuntary laugh. It was having the right effect, he thought.

Then she turned her face up to him, with a look of sharp anguish.

'What is it?' he said with alarm.

'I want to be your mistress,' she said. 'I want you to take me as your mistress.'

There was a moment of stunned silence.

'But that is impossible,' he said at last, in a hoarse whisper. 'Impossible.' At the same time, however, his mind became a tumult of conflict, of guilt and temptation, of tenderness, of terrified desire. She had her arms around him now and pulled herself against him. He felt the softness of her body under her gown and could smell her hair and the perfume of soap or scent from her skin. He felt a gulf opening into which he could easily and gladly fall.

He realised that he was holding her more and more closely, more and more caressively. Her face turned upwards to him, with softened eyes, smiling, offering herself to be kissed.

And it was then that enormity of it all finally took hold of him and breaking away, he stepped back. 'This would be wrong,' he said, as gently as he could. 'It would not make you happy. Perhaps much worse. Much, much worse.'

He backed towards the door, looking at the now pathetic figure in the centre of the room, her hands still half gesturing towards him, her face streaming with tears, and then let himself out into the corridor.

6

Chapter 6

Anna, Leeds, 2010

I knew when Stella phoned me to say that Rob, my son, was coming back from London for a couple of days that something was afoot. It was difficult enough getting Rob to come back home at the best of times, and when I'd told him on the phone that I was leaving his father, he was pretty blunt about it, to say the least. I could not imagine him merrily tripping back at this point in time unless someone had been leaning on him.

I waited.

Sure enough, two days later, there came another call from Stella.

'I mentioned that Rob was coming up here, didn't I?'

'Yes,' I said as non-committally as I could manage.

'Well, he's here.'

'With you?'

'Yes. Well, not at this precise moment. Guy's taken him to the pub. But yes, he's staying here. Tonight, anyway.'

I waited for what this was building up to.

'So, anyway, the thing is...' she continued, with obvious tentativeness, 'the thing is, dad thinks we should all get together, you know, whilst he's here, have, you know, a sort of family gathering...'

'That sounds jolly!'

'You know,' she went on, ignoring my sarcasm, 'chat things through, sort of thing.'

I took a long breath and let it out as silently as I could. At what point does firmness on your own behalf become callousness towards your children, and therefore a dilemma? Martin knew this.

'And where is this pow-wow supposed to take place?' I asked.

'At home. You know, I mean home in Leeds.'

'I see,' I said.

'You will come, won't you mum?'

I knew, as she explained the details – Martin had clearly planned it all out – that I had no choice.

I spent the next twenty-four hours organising my defence, so to speak. It was no good, I knew, me using the same kind of terminology that Madeline used when talking about my divorce; I did not want to justify my decision to leave Martin by reference to his controlling be-haviour, not in front of his children, for sure, and it probably wouldn't work anyway, because Martin would be ready to diminish my argu-ments and make them seem ridiculous. I had to try, somehow, to frame it all in a positive way, to explain that I had simply come to a point in my life when I needed to move forward. It was as if a rehearsal was go-ing on in my mind all the time, trying out phrases, thinking of compar-isons, formulating expressions and then testing them out to see if they sounded true. In the end, I crossed and recrossed the territory so many times that I hardly knew what I was going to say. I would just have to 'wing it', as Jenny would say.

Just to get my mind away from it for a while, I went back to the bits of information I had gathered on Christina Tasse. I had printed some of them off and put them in a Nirex; I went through them to see if there was anything I might have missed. Then I went back to my inter-net searches, which was confusing at first because I couldn't remember which ones I'd paid the fee for. However, I did get a little bit more. The last census information was from 1911, but there was a National Regis-ter in 1939, presumably something to do with the war, and I managed to track Christina and her mother on that, both at an address in Horsforth. I also came across a very short epitaph for Christina in a local newspaper from April 1971. I was hoping I might find something more personal, like mentions in letters or diaries, but no such luck.

When I woke up the next morning, however, Christina was far from my mind, and I had that anxious feeling that I knew I was going to carry with me all through the day at work. Co-incidentally that day, I had a call from my landlord reminding me that I would have to let him know by the end of the week if I wanted to extend the lease on my apartment for another six months. I say co-incidentally, though it did occur to me that Martin might well have calculated this himself and might well have timed the family get-together to be ahead of the game.

I drove there from work just after six o'clock, with the only mantra in my mind being 'stay calm, stay firm'. I was glad that none of the neighbours were about, or did not seem to be, though in my heightened self-consciousness, I imagined at least a couple of them, peeping from windows at the return of the prodigal!

Stella's car was already on the drive. Martin's, of course, would be in the garage. I parked in front of Stella, quickly checked my make-up in the mirror, and then walked towards the front door, with the overwhelming feeling that I was walking into a trap.

It was very strange entering the house I had left all those months before, and not a little daunting. I felt like an intruder. All the familiar objects, the furniture, the wallpaper, the lamps seemed to be looking at me suspiciously as if slightly disdainful of my return, and I have to admit that my stomach was churning.

Rob was sitting in the armchair by the window, his knees wide apart and his hands crossed over his stomach. He had put on a little weight, I noticed, and with my mother's instinct, perhaps a little odd in the circumstances, I was glad because I'd never been convinced that he fed himself properly. Stella was sitting forward on the settee, smiling but looking on tenterhooks. I was glad that she had not brought Guy. Martin was in his usual armchair at the side of the mantlepiece. I sat down at the other end of the settee from Stella. Strangely – or perhaps not so – we had all gravitated to the positions we had adopted in the past when watching television together, a sort of territorial atavism, I suppose.

'So,' said Martin, slowly, almost affably rubbing his hands together, 'Who's for a drink? Beer Rob?'

Rob made a single nod of the head.

'Stella?'

'Just a coffee for me. I'm driving later.'

'Same for me,' I chipped in quickly.

'Right. Do you want to make it then, darling?'

I wasn't sure whether this was addressed to Stella or a casually reconditioned endearment for me, but Stella saved any requirement for clarification by getting up briskly and going into the kitchen.

'Are you all right?' I asked Rob, sotto voce, as the other two were sorting out the drinks, trying to connect, despite the situation, at a maternal level.

'Yes,' he replied. 'Why should I not be?'

Five minutes later, we were all back in position, with our drinks to hand.

'Well,' said Martin, 'it's a while since we've all sat down together like this.'

'Gran's funeral,' said Rob, and somehow we all managed to laugh.

'Or how about when Stella told us she was going to shack up with another dentist?' said Martin.

'Guy was here then,' said Stella.

'Of course he was.'

'And I wasn't here,' Rob added.

'Weren't you? Right. Must have been thinking of another time. Same number, anyhow. Guy must have been sitting where you are now.'

'The time I remember,' said Stella, 'is when they cancelled our flight to Jamaica at the last minute, and we sat here, with our suitcases packed in the hall, wondering what we could do about it.'

'And I got onto Leeds-Bradford,' said Martin, 'and they fixed us up with an internal to Gatwick and hey presto!'

'You were the hero, dad,' said Rob, with a flatness of intonation that might not even have been sarcastic.

'Jamaica!' said Martin, choosing not to notice anything, subtle or otherwise, in Rob's tone. 'What a holiday that turned out to be in the end!'

And so it went on, for nearly half an hour. Reminiscences, anecdotes, almost like a family album. I couldn't tell whether this was a deliberate ploy on Martin's part, or just the natural way we were avoiding the elephant in the room.

It was Rob who was the first to break the artificial calm. 'Look,' he said impatiently, 'is somebody going to tell me when we're going to get on with this, or are we just going to keep waffling on all night.'

'Don't talk to your mother like that!' said Martin, which struck me as being strange, as Rob, so far as I was aware, had not addressed his remark directly to me. 'Can't you appreciate what a mess she is in?'

I saw where he was going with it now.

'Well, I thought we were going to talk about it,' said Rob. 'That's what I've been dragged all the way up from London for, isn't it?'

This admission of involuntariness on his part did not surprise me.

'Yes,' said Stella, coming in quickly as if to cover for him. 'To have a talk, to try to sort something out. So we can all get on with our lives.'

I nearly said that I was already getting on with mine, but I held my tongue.

'I'm an open book,' said Martin. 'I'm prepared to talk about anything. Maybe your mum's the one who finds it difficult to address it.'

'Mum?' Stella enquired, with that hurt softness she has, the one I used to have. I was about to unleash one of my rehearsed lines, the one about when you look in a mirror and suddenly ask, for the first time, who am I, who is that person, but I didn't think it would cut any ice; quite the opposite, it might give Martin the chance to throw in one of his favourite dismissive terms, like flim-flam or twaddle, or his very favourite: per-lease!

'Look,' said Martin, now addressing me directly rather than working through the kids. 'We've been in this together, right from the start, right from the start, and on to the end, that's how it should be. I've made mistakes, God only knows I'm aware of that. I haven't been perfect. But this? How did it come to this, that's what I'm asking myself right now. And I don't know what the answer is, I truly don't.'

'Mum?' said Stella again, tears now streaming down her face.

How could I answer this? Once again, all my bits of rehearsed flim-flam deserted me. I knew from that moment that I was going to capitulate.

Martin now upped his game, saying how much it meant to him to keep the family together, how much he regretted it if he had undervalued me or taken me for granted, saying, almost with a tearful edge in his voice how great it would be if we could put the whole daft thing behind us and move on. You could say he was playing a blinder!

And like the cosy feeling you sometimes get after two or three glasses of wine, softening the edges of reality and providing you with a fuzzy kind of insulation, I began to see the good side of it. I would be able to forget all the nasty business of going through a divorce, I could release my children from this burden, as they saw it, of having a renegade mother, I could come back to the relative luxury of my own home, I could even stay here tonight. Perhaps Martin was even banking on that.

'Sod it, I'm going to get another beer,' said Rob.

'I'll get it for you,' I said, giving myself a brief stay of execution from the climb-down that was about to come.

'Stella?'

'A small glass of white, please. I mean, really small, please mum.'

I went into the kitchen, immediately remembering where everything was.

Martin followed me in.

'It's up to you completely,' he said, as I opened the bottle of beer for Rob. 'If you're determined, well, go for it.'

I poured Stella's glass of wine.

'I'll take these through,' I said, not knowing whether I was being halted in my tracks or not. Two minutes later and I would have been saying, right, I've decided to stay, or something to that effect; probably still was going to say that.

I handed Rob his beer.

'Cheers,' gruffly.

'Thanks, mum,' said Stella, with a sweet smile as if I had performed some exceptional service.

I knew they were now expecting Martin and I to come to a rapid conclusion in the kitchen and then reappear to announce it.

Martin had poured himself another glass of red wine. I followed suit with Stella and gave myself a small white. It could be a large one later, if it came to it.

'As I said, go for it if you must,' Martin resumed, now leaning casually against the work surface. 'But if you do, I mean, if you insist on it, we will have to sell the cottage in Staithes. Your solicitor has told you that hasn't he?'

'She,' I corrected.

Martin threw his head back in mirth. 'I might have known.'

I waited for him to explain.

'Well, the arithmetic is fairly simple,' he said. 'As far as the house is concerned, this house, I mean, I've no intention of buying you out. If you want to buy me out... well unless there's a lot I don't know, which is unlikely, you will need to sell the cottage to raise the funds for that. And remember, we re-mortgaged here five years ago, so not all the equity is ours. Also, of course, remember that legally the cottage is half mine.'

'But it was left to me...'

He shrugged his shoulders. 'As I say, legally, half of it is mine.'

'And what if I don't want to buy you out?'

Again, he shrugged his shoulders. 'Well, then the house would go up for sale, and you would get your share minus my share of the Staithes cottage. You have to be realistic about what you could afford to buy, unless you mean to live in rented accommodation forever.'

I tried to remember what Madeline had said about the 60-40 split, and tried to adjust the vague picture of how exactly I was expecting things to be after the divorce. But I had no head for the figures. I had always relied on Martin for that, or, more recently, Madeline.

And in a way, it didn't matter.

And Martin would never know how effectively, in that brief conversation in the kitchen, he had snatched defeat out of the jaws of victory.

I can't remember much after that. I swallowed my wine, said a brief goodbye to the children, and said thanks for coming. Then I made a hasty retreat before the tears started.

Funnily enough, it was Rob who followed me to the car. He put his hand on my shoulder. 'Take care, mum,' he said. 'Let me know if you need anything.'

Well, the tears came readily after that, and lasted all the way home with attendant snuffles and sobs. But it was done. There was literally no going back now, and I knew it was the right thing.

7

Chapter 7

C hristina, Leeds, 1910

It was a damp November evening, and as the car passed through Headingly, the bell of St Michael's announced the hour with eight sombre notes. The car moved on through Hyde Park, then past Woodhouse Moor before beginning the gradual descent towards the city.

'Turn here,' she instructed the driver.

The car turned into Back Blenheim Terrace.

'Here,' she said, indicating, to the left, a three-storey brick building in the Georgian style. 'Stop here.'

'Right, Miss.'

'Will you pick me up here at ten o'clock?'

'Yes, Miss.'

'Be sure you're not late.'

As the car pulled away, she stood for a moment, looking at the steps and the rail up to the doorway. She had not been here for seven years. Now, two years after the end of the war, the 18th November, 1920, the studio of James Redfern, was to be the venue for the reformation of the Steers Club, closed since the start of hostilities.

James Redfern was a respected portrait and landscape artist, a notable raconteur, known for his sociable habits and hospitality, and the Steers Club, of which he was a founding member, had been meeting since the turn of the century to converse about the arts and to enjoy a little in the way conviviality. Her previous visit had been not as a member of the club, which, though not officially so, was, in fact, an all-male affair, but to mark the occasion of one of her canvases being hung in the city gallery. Charles Penner, of course, had been one of those present.

From the vestibule, a stairway led to the first floor where James Redfern had his studio. The wallpaper, a dull pink, was the same, she recalled, and at the top of the stairs, a portrait of Lord Tennyson was hung above an aspidistra in a brown pot, and next to it a settee in the Empire style, with faded burgundy upholstery and gold tassels. A low murmur of voices came from the open door to the studio, and as she entered, she was greeted by one or two polite nods.

She recalled that there had been somewhere between thirty and forty people present at that last meeting, and though there had been serious mutterings about the possibility of war, the atmosphere had been decidedly jolly. On this occasion, there were far fewer, and the theme of numerous conversations, she soon realised, was how many of the members had been 'lost'.

She was recognised and greeted by Max Long, who had been a fellow student at the Art School fifteen years before. He came across the room with a look of relief on his face and fetched a glass of sherry for them both.

'Pretty glum here!' he announced. 'I was beginning to wonder about sloping off until I saw you.'

'How are you, Max?'

'Pretty well, on the whole, yes.'

'Did you...'

'If you are going to ask me if I fought, then I shall have to disappoint you. Lungs, I'm afraid. TB as a child. More's the pity. You went up to Staithes, didn't you, with Penner?'

'Yes.'

'Lucky girl.'

'And what have you been up to then?'

'Family business. Furniture, don't you know? A bit of dabbling and daubing now and then, but nothing serious. Not sure why they invited me, really.'

'Me neither. Is he here?'

'Who? Penner?'

'Yes.'

'Don't think so. Haven't seen him at any rate.'

She was disappointed. The invitation was not signed, but she guessed that it might have been at his instigation that she was asked.

A gramophone had been brought into the room, and a crackly and slightly wobbly record of a Chopin piano sonata was played. She made an excuse to move on from Max, and looked at some of Redfern's paintings, some hung around the walls, some leaning up against them, some on easels. A good few she recognised as having been here before. They were mainly landscapes in the old style, evoking English rural scenes, and portraits of the mid-Victorian era, impressive but very old-fashioned. Robert himself, who she could now see talking to a group on the far side, must be in his seventies or even eighties, now. She guessed that he had not produced much new work for some time. Should she go over and introduce herself, she wondered; would he even remember who she was?

There was a sound of some implement being tapped against a glass, the clearing of a throat, and the muttering fell quickly to silence. Robert Redfern made a brief welcome, and then handed on to someone else, whom he referred to as Lionel, though it was not someone she recognised. Lionel, it seemed, was being proposed as the new chairman of the group. He spoke in a desultory way, echoing the sentiments of loss they must all feel, and mentioning some names in particular. Then he went on to set out a prospectus for the reformed group. It was low key, not quite getting away from the feeling of despondency everyone seemed to be feeling, but it was at least something. He finished and there was muted applause, and then Robert Redfern, asked for a show of hands approving his chairmanship.

'There. I think that will do,' he announced, and there was another ripple of polite applause. In the silence which followed, someone put a rag-time record on the gramophone, no doubt in an attempt to chivvy up the spirits.

She sighed inwardly, wishing that she had asked the driver to return at nine o'clock and not ten. Then she felt a tap on her shoulder. She turned. It was Charles, and she saw, in an instant, that in the five years since she had seen him last, age and ill health had taken their toll. His hair, always thick and full, had receded almost to the crown and his complexion, characteristically ruddy from the wind and the sun, was now noticeably pallid. He took her hand and brought it to his lips.

'Christina! My dear! I am so, so glad you could come.'

She smiled and squeezed his hand, feeling a tear form in the corner of her eye.

'Come, let us get away from this execrable noise and find somewhere to talk.'

They walked to the landing and sat at the settee, and he took her hand again.

'Let me look at you!' he said. 'Ha! Beautiful as ever. I shall paint you again, just as you are now.' He looked at her with almost the same intensity she had noticed when doing that first portrait ten years before, but now the look had a mournful tinge.

'But how about you?' she asked. 'If you don't mind me saying so, you don't look quite well.'

'Well, there's no point in hiding it. I have developed what the doctor tells me is a heart condition. I get quickly short of breath. And fatigued easily too. I fear my days of wandering miles with my easel are in the past.'

'But you are still painting?'

'Oh yes, what else would I do with my wretched life?'

'In Staithes? Sandsend?'

'Yes. Dear old Sandsend. We have our own house there now. Managed to buy some land, just after the war finished. I spend almost all my time there now. This a rare visit to Leeds.'

'And how is Mrs Penner? And the children.'

'Mrs Penner, yes, well, quite well. The children all flown now, of course. But you must come to visit us. Whenever you can,' he added, his voice trailing off a little.

A couple of fellows holding tea cups and saucers came out onto the landing, and exchanged greetings, staying to chat for a moment.

'Tea in there if you're thirsty,' said one of them.

Charles looked to Christina.

'No, thank you,' she replied.

The man smiled and bowed his head slightly, then the two of them moved aside, leaving them in private again.

'My brother Henry was killed in the war, you know,' she now said.

'Yes,' he said almost in a whisper.

'In 1916. We don't know quite where, or exactly when. Probably on the Somme. Just that he was killed, really, that's all we know. No body or anything.'

'How terrible. Your parents must have been...'

'Yes. Devastated. My father especially. He encouraged him to enlist you see. Thought it a matter of duty. I don't think my mother ever forgave him for that. He died two years ago. Maybe you knew that also?'

He nodded his head, once slowly, then several times quickly. She found herself suppressing a sob.

'And how is your mother?'

'She suffers badly from her nerves. It was all I could do to persuade her to let me come here tonight. She has lost so much. She has a terror of letting me out of her sight. For fear of losing me too.'

'Understandable...' he said, and then after a moment, squeezing her hand again, 'but you must live your own life too. How old are you now?'

'Twenty-nine.'

'You must live your life.'

'I sometimes wonder if any of us is really allowed to live our own life,' she said. 'Even when we think we are doing, it's maybe just an illusion.'

'Yes. Maybe so.'

There was a pause of some length.

'Do you remember our trip to Bruges?' she asked, at last.

'Yes, and Paris.'

'You showed me something someone had sketched on a serviette.'

'In Paris, yes. Picasso.'

'Yes, I thought it was. I couldn't quite remember.'

'He is quite famous now. '

'Yes, I know.'

'And growing more so.'

'I read about an exhibition of some of his work at Leicester.'

'Yes. I toyed with the idea of going to see it, but in the end I didn't. Too much trouble to find that I still don't understand him. Perhaps even less so now than then.'

'I'm sorry I didn't meet him.'

'Yes. I wish you had. It was a strange night, all in all.'

'The night when I offered myself to you.'

'Yes,' he said with a kind of dry wistfulness.

'What a silly confused girl I was.'

The conversation paused, as if it had reached a point from which it could go no further.

'And what a silly confused man I was,' he said at last.

She laughed. 'Why do you say that? You only did what was right.'

'Yes.'

'You said it would lead to unhappiness.'

'And so it would,' he said with a catch in his throat, 'but what happiness have we had, any of us, since then?'

She did not reply.

'I have often thought of that evening,' he continued. 'Yes, knowing that I did the right thing. But in truth I think I was afraid of my own desire. If I had the chance again, I think I would have held you closer than life itself. And had I known what was to follow, those dreadful war years, I would not have turned down such a chance that life offered me.'

'The war has changed everything. No-one can go back to what things were like then.'

'How gloomy we are being.'

'That year. When I came to Staithes for the first time, that was when I thought I was living my own life. Never since, not really. Do you remember that little studio I had, in the village?'

'How could I forget? I had to bring you food every day. I don't think you even knew how to make a pot of tea!'

'Well, that's true, but I didn't care about such trivial things. But I walked out every morning, with my bag and my easel, and I felt as free as a bird, and as happy, if birds are happy.'

'Let's agree that they probably are.'

'I remember walking all the way along until the path brought me to a place just above the bay, looking down on the sands. I imagined it full of people, and in my mind, I composed a picture which expressed the pure happiness I was feeling, but expressed through the people in the picture, children who were dancing hand in hand.'

'You never told me of that canvas.'

'I wanted to finish it and show it you complete. Of course, I never did complete it.'

'But you must.'

'I don't know if I can ever finish it now. I can see the scene and the people, but I can never imagine feeling again the emotion I felt then. I fear it would be lifeless.'

He patted her hand. 'You are still young. Time is on your side. It will come back. Just as you must promise to come back to see us there.'

'I will. Perhaps when mother is feeling more herself. Perhaps then.'

'Don't let life close in around you, Christina.'

'I will try not to.'

'Promise!'

She smiled and squeezed his hand. 'What happened to the serviette?' she asked. 'Did you keep it?'

'I can't remember,' he said, furrowing his brow. 'No. I don't think I did. I must have thrown it in the bin.'

The corner of his eye crinkled into a grin, and then they both began to laugh.

8

Chapter 8

Anna & Christina, Staithes

After the family gathering, I took a day off work and that was a mistake, because if I felt a little bit blue in the morning, by the end of the afternoon I was feeling thoroughly depressed.

I phoned Stella thinking that she would still be upset, but in fact she was quite upbeat. 'It was worth a try,' she said in a practical tone, 'but at least we've cleared the air.'

'Yes,' I agreed, though I wasn't quite sure what she meant.

'We all know where we stand. Just have to get on with it.'

'Is Rob OK?'

'Oh, yes. I drove him to the station this morning. He was quite chatty, unlike him. I think he might have a girlfriend down there.'

'Really?'

'Yes. Just something he said to Guy.'

'Oh well. I mean, good, though I expect we'll be the last to know. Did you say anything to dad?'

'No. He shooed us off pretty soon after you went.'

'How was he?' I asked, feeling that I should, though I didn't really want to hear the answer.

'Oh, he'll be all right. He's coming over here at the weekend. Going to go out for a round of golf with Guy.'

'Oh good,' I said.

The phone-call made me feel better on one level at least. It seemed clear that they were all going to get on pretty well without me, and I had to count that a plus, all things considered.

I could easily have become a bit maudlin again, but I resolved not to. Instead, I opened a bottle of wine, took out a notepad and started to work out my finances. I did a bit of looking around on Rightmove to get an idea of what the house would be worth and did a bit of guesswork about the value of the Staithes cottage, both to sell and as an on-going investment. Then I did a bit of dividing up by percentages, because Martin's veiled threat, parading as friendly advice, *you have to be realistic about what you can afford to buy, unless you mean to live in rented accommodation forever*, was definitely sticking in my mind. It had never really occurred to me that he would claim a share of the cottage in Staithes, and I curse my own naivety in not being properly aware of how much of the equity in the house was actually ours. I vaguely remembered Martin talking about the re-mortgage, but exactly why we'd done it – or exactly why he'd done it - I had no idea.

At the end of the evening, and three glasses of wine later, I had several wildly differing estimates of how much money I would be able to call my own when the divorce was finalised, and I had to find somewhere permanent to live. I was going to have to get serious in my discussions with Madeline, I decided, it was all getting to be pretty heavy grown-up stuff.

I called her the next morning from work, but she was out of the office, not due back until after the weekend. I made an appointment for Monday, and then, because I couldn't bear the thought of stewing about in it for two days in the flat, I decided to drive up to Staithes.

It was a warm summer evening when I arrived. Standing at the bedroom window, I saw that below, on the roof of the porch, a seagull was nursing three chicks in her nest. They were funny fluffy speckled little things, quite capable of strutting around and falling off if she didn't monitor them constantly. I watched for some time and realised that there were several other nesting pairs on the nearby rooftops, all with their little brood. The males tended to be perched on the chimney pots, like sentries on duty, taking a moment off now and then to have a natter or a moan.

When I had unpacked, I went for a walk over 'the bridge of sighs', as I had christened it, and then made my way back and along to the pub and I was glad to see that Arnold was there. I joined him at him at a table outside and ordered a drink and a snack.

The tide was fully in, and just below where we were sitting, teenage boys were jumping off the harbour wall into the water.

'They must have skin like leather,' I said. 'It must be freezing.'

'Or lots of blubber!'

The waiter brought my order, and I started.

'How's it going, then?' he asked in his usual slightly saturnine way.

'OK,' I said.

He tipped his head one way as if to say that he wouldn't probe any further if that's what I wanted.

'How's the fishing?' I asked.

'OK,' he said, 'yes, been good, usually gets better this time of year, the fish come back, you know, as the sea warms up a bit. Not like in the old days when it was teeming with them, but enough. Makes it worthwhile. Some lobsters too.'

'I didn't know you caught lobsters.'

'Got a few baskets,' he said. 'If you ever have lobster here, good chance it might be one of mine.'

'I shall order it next time,' I said.

We both laughed, and it was then, or rather after we got another drink in, that I decided to tell him about my situation, give him the full picture, that is.

He was a patient listener, very non-judgemental, just nodding his head, and twisting his mouth a little now and then as if weighing things up.

Of course, you always mediate things when you present yourself to someone else, don't you? No one wants to show themselves in a bad light, light, I suppose, but I tried not to present myself as a victim, or, on the other hand, to 'big' myself up in any way. When I told him about the meeting with Martin and the kids, he twisted his mouth a little more, so that I could tell he judged it a ploy to trap me, but then I remembered, of course, that he had children too, and might be setting one transparency over another, so to speak. I moved it on to my appointment with Madeline, who I'd introduced at an earlier part of the tale.

'Sounds as if you've done the right thing,' he said, when I pause and sat back with my drink.

'Do you think so?'

'You have to keep moving,' he said. 'Even if you stay put, you have to find a way of moving. Sounds like you didn't have one.'

'No,' I said. 'That's what it felt like. Of course, I may have to sell the cottage.'

'How so?'

I explained, in broad terms, what the bits of the equation were. He didn't offer any comment. I got the feeling that he simply had no idea of dealing with sums and figures of that magnitude.

'Well,' he said, at last, 'you've just got to take it one step at a time.'

'Put one foot in front of the other, 'I came back with.

We both laughed. 'We sometimes talk such rubbish, don't we?' I said, and then, thinking it was time to change the subject, 'oh, I meant to tell you. I found out a little bit more about Christina.'

'Really?'

'Well, just a bit. And about Charles Penner. He died in 1924.'

'Really?'

'Yes. From a heart attack.'

Arnold nodded.

'Her brother died in the First World War and her father died in 1918.'

'A lot of deaths you've found out for me!'

'And more. Christina's mother lived until 1941, and of course, as we know, Christina herself died in 1971.'

'Quite old, then.'

'Eighty odd. And the thing is, so far as I can tell, she lived in the same house all that time, and in the 1939 register her mother lives at that address too. And there's no record at all of her ever getting married.'

'Lucky girl, maybe.'

'Well, I wondered whether she might have got married abroad, or something, but then I found a tiny obituary in the local paper where it refers to her as a spinster.'

'I bet she wouldn't have liked that. She would have preferred 'artist'.'

'Well, it mentions that too. But it definitely refers to her as Miss Tasse. I mean, I know she might have kept that as a professional name, but if she was married or a widow, you would have thought they'd have mentioned her married name.'

'Maybe so.'

'Do you want to know what my theory is?'

'Go on.'

'Well, brother dies in the trenches, father dies soon after the war. I think she stayed at home and looked after her mother.'

'Until 1941.'

'Yes. By which time she would have been around fifty, possibly a bit late to think of getting married then. Plus the fact that she stayed in the same house.'

'So, what conclusion do you draw then?'

'Well, I think poor Christina probably led a very lonely life.'

'Unless she was gay.'

'Do you think?'

'Well, it wasn't as public then as it is now, I guess, but we know it went on. I mean, it wasn't invented in 1969. Has to be a possibility.'

I thought about this, not knowing whether I wanted it to be a possibility or not.

'I suppose we'll never know,' I concluded.

When we left the pub it was still a pleasant night. We walked along the main street and onto the bridge where I had been before.

'I call this the Bridge of Sighs,' I said. 'As in Venice.'

'Sounds very romantic.'

'Well, not really. The prisoners sighed as it was their last glimpse of the world before being executed.'

'Oh, well, in that case!'

We walked back. Outside the Royal George, a few people were sitting out with their drinks. It was still warm, but the light was just beginning to fade.

'Would you like to come back?' I asked, when we reached the Barrass Steps. It wasn't on impulse. At some point I had made my mind up.

He shuffled a little uncomfortably, but I could tell he knew what I meant.

'Would you?'

'Yes,' he muttered. 'I suppose... yes.'

I didn't take his apparent reticence for reluctance.

'Come on then,' I said, slipping my arm into his.' Let's see if we're both still up to it.'

When I awoke, later, in the early hours, Arnold had gone. He had slipped out and away without disturbing me. I was both glad and sorry. It hadn't been perfect. Far from it. But there was a sense in which, all the potential for awkwardness having now once been faced, it might have been nice to wake up next to him in the morning and who knows...? Glad, too, though, because it was, after all, somehow easier to wake up alone, and just to have one's own thoughts.

I went back to sleep quite quickly. The next thing I knew it was dawn, and at first, I thought he had returned and was sitting at the end of the bed. But it wasn't him. It was the figure I had seen, on that first visit, at the end of the alley. The same figure, too, I assumed who had come upstairs, albeit invisibly, and who had sung a childish ditty preparing for bed. It was the figure not of a child, however, but of a young woman, of perhaps twenty, with very dark hair, which she was tying up into a bun behind, and wearing a white blouse.

'Christina?' I whispered.

Immediately, she turned and smiled at me, still holding her hair behind in both hands, and then she stood, as if to say, *come on, it's time to go.*

She waited for me as I dressed.

If she was ghost, she wasn't as I had ever imagined one. There was no ghastly pallor or shimmering light. Nor could I see through a spectre-like thinness of ectoplasm. She seemed completely corporeal, and I felt sure that if I reached over, she would actually be there to touch, but of course I didn't try.

When I was ready, she led the way downstairs. I put on my coat, and she tied a cloak around her shoulders. Then she picked up a leather bag, the one I had seen her with that first time, and a piece of equipment that I now identified as an easel. I saw, as we went out, that there was no bolt on the door, just the latch. It all seemed to make perfect sense.

We crossed the bottom of the village and made our way along Church Street to the point where it became a lane, and then a steep track. We walked on, she always a few paces ahead of me, until we came to the farm, and then we carried on towards the cliff path.

I remembered the wind and the wild sea that day when I first reached this point. Now the sea was calm, with just a hint of white on the tips of the waves as they came into the bay. She stopped and waited for me to come alongside her. Together, we looked down to village from where we'd just come, looking toy-like below in the light of a fresh sun that was just rising from the horizon. Then, she looked at me, and smiled again, before setting out once more along the cliff path.

Around the path, the vegetation had grown a lot since my first walk all those weeks ago. At times I was looking at the sea through tall waving grasses, and on the landward side of the paths fields of barley were now reaching their bearded maturity, whilst further along, purplish brown grasses gave the sweeping meadows a tint and texture which I seemed to recognise from paintings I had seen. The gorse was now fading, but there was still a scent of the hawthorn in bloom, and floppy wild roses posed in the hedges. There was a lot of cow parsley and foxgloves, and other flowers I partly recognised, and whose names I might once have known, though I couldn't be specific about them now.

Christina was taking me, I realised, finally, to the spot I had reached on my first walk, two months before, the spot where I had had a strange sense, without being able to pin it down, of having been before. Here, she stopped and set up her easel, arranged her brushes and palette, and began to work.

I sat down on the same slab of rock as before and took in the scene. It was becoming, now, a beautiful morning, but on the beach below there was not a soul in sight. Nor did anyone come past, in either direction, from the path. Without going to stand behind her to watch, I tried to work out what she was painting. A landscape, presumably, since there were no people - the span of the beach, the wide arc of the sea, the distant line of cliffs, the sky above with its playful fleecy clouds.

After a while, I admit, I began to wonder how long we were going to be there. And did she want me to stay? Would she be offended, I wondered, if I were to take my leave. I suppose I could have explained that I had to drive back to Leeds at some point, but somehow that seemed completely out of keeping.

I don't recall how long it was before I heard the little snatch of child-like singing but when I turned towards her she was wiping her brush with a rag and then she turned to me with a pleased smile that seemed to be saying, it's finished, come and have a look.

I stood up from my rock and went to stand behind her. I don't know if there had been anything on the canvas to begin with or whether she had started from scratch. If the latter, she had worked with incredible speed as what I now saw was a completed painting. And it was not a landscape, either, as I had imagined; true, it was the beach and the sea and the distant cliffs, but the beach itself was full of people in all the bright and light colours people wear for the beach. In particular, at the centre of the canvas, and its obvious focus, were two children who seemed to be dancing with sheer joy at being where they were.

'You've painted that from my imagination,' I said, 'or rather, you've painted it from my memory...'

She leaned back and looked up at me, seeming very pleased, and gave me another winsome smile.

I looked at the painting again and then out towards the scene. And I saw that the beach was now no longer empty but peopled exactly as she had captured them in the painting. I walked forward to look at it from the edge of the eminence which was our viewpoint. Some of the people were reclining on sunbeds or deckchairs, some on rugs spread out on the sand. One of them, a man, was reading a newspaper, and I suddenly recognised him as my father. Then the whole scene came back to me. I could even remember the place on the lane where he had parked our car, an old pale blue Ford Escort, and the way my mother had brought a picnic and was trying to protect it from the sand that the childish dancers were kicking up. And the dancer, the one in the blue dress, was me, and the other a friend who had been allowed to come on holiday with us; and just as in Christina's painting, we were dancing for joy.

When at last I turned back, meaning to tell her, through the film of my tears, how grateful I was, she had gone. Gone, along with the easel and the leather bag and all the rest of her equipment. But I knew, as surely as possible, that once, maybe a long time ago, she had sat in this spot and painted such a picture, and that she had brought me here specially to see it, and to remember.

As I was driving out of the village, later, I saw Arnold standing there, and I stopped and wound down the window.

'Will I see you again?' he asked.

'I've got a couple of bookings over the next few weeks,' I replied.

'Getting to be that time of year, I guess.'

'Yes.'

'Well, it's a small place. I'll know if you're here.'

'Yes.'

He grinned. 'And if you decide to sell up, well, I guess I'll know that, too.'

I caught sight of him in the mirror as I rounded the corner, his hand raised in a provisional farewell.

The end

John's Yorkshire Titles

John's Yorkshire titles include:

Enoch's Hammer - A tale of the Yorkshire Luddites

The House on Lady Hall lane - a dark romance

The Gallery - a Detective Nula Ryan murder mystery tale

Marcia - a bitter-sweet coming-of-age romance set in the decades following WW2

Evelyn - a tale of love, war, absence and family life, set during WW2

Canky's Trade - set in 1812, a tale of the resurrectionists or 'graver-obbers'

Joss - a coming-of-age story based on the diary of a fourteen year-old girl who is displaced to Middleton to live with a strange aunt, set in the 1950s

Consequences - set in the 1980s, an ill-fated teenage romance leading to unimaginable consequences - a novel of love and survival

Finding Josie - when Nick Roberts returns to Middleton for the funeral of an old friend, he is haunted by memories of his first love, Josie, and finding her becomes his obsession

Idlers Corner - a tale of the great Middleton flood of 1927

About the Author

John Wheatley was born and brought up in Middleton, near Oldham, and was educated in Manchester and at Leeds University.

He was a teacher of English for many years, in Kent and the North West, but then, in a dramatic mid-career shift, became qualified as a Plumbing and Heating engineer!

He has written sixteen novels, set mainly in Yorkshire, Anglesey and his home town of Middleton.

Mot of the stories have a historical setting, reflecting his interest in events of the nineteenth and early twentieth century, though also dealing with the more recent history of the late twentieth and early twenty-first centuries.

JOHN'S ANGLESEY TITLES

Flowers of Vitriol, set during the copper boom at Parys Mountain, Amlwch, 1817

The Weeping Sands - set mainly in Beaumaris, Anglesey in 1831, but with time shifts to the English Civil War and the present

A Golden Mist - set mainly in Moelfre, Anglesey, dealing with the wreck of the gold bullion ship, *The Royal Charter* in the great storm of 1859

The Papers of Matthew Locke - set in Rhosneigr in 1883, a romantic fantasy time shift story

The Exile's Daughter - as love story set in Church Bay, Anglesey and various battle zones of WW1